MARK & KATHRYN DONNELLY

An Emberlyn's Tale

This book was professionally typeset on Reedsy.
Find out more at reedsy.com

Contents

Chapter 1

In the quiet village of Everwood, nestled at the edge of a vast and mysterious forest, the townsfolk lived with a secret fear. They whispered tales of the shadowy woods, and the presence of a malicious shaman named Malachar. This sinister figure had cast a spell over the forest, and its darkness loomed, casting a pall over the village. It was a place that few dared to enter.

Everwood was a quaint little village, a few days' travel from any major towns. The folks here were simple. They had a bakery, an apothecary, and the market square. The village, nestled among the once-vibrant woods, now stood as a weary sentinel of centuries gone by. The forest that had once burst forth with a symphony of colors had lost its vitality. The branches of the ancient trees, gnarled and twisted, loomed overhead like silent witnesses to the passing of time.

The farmland, once a fertile expanse of green and gold, was now a desolate wasteland, where rows of withered stalks stood in the barren Earth. The land, once yielding a bounty of crops, now bore only the scars of countless harvests and the weight of forgotten toil. The very soil seemed weary, as if it had given all it could and now awaited respite.

The town itself, with its cobblestone streets and weathered buildings, spoke of a history that stretched back through the ages. Yet, the facades were marred by the ravages of time, their once vibrant colors faded to muted shades of gray and brown. The windows of the old buildings gazed out onto a world that had moved on. The roofs, covered in moss and lichen, seemed to sag under the weight of the years. It was a place where the past and the present coexisted, where the whispers of history could be heard.

In this village, there lived a young girl named Elara. She was like a slender birch tree standing tall in a moonlit forest, her fair complexion resembling the pale, silvery bark of the tree. Her eyes, the color of a clear summer sky, glistened like sapphires, revealing the intelligence that sparkled within. Long strands of reddish-brown hair cascaded like the finest strands of auburn silk, shimmering in the sunlight like the leaves of autumn.

Her caring nature was a gentle stream, always flowing with compassion and warmth, nurturing those around her like the forest's underbrush sheltering delicate flowers. Her kindness, like the soft rustling of leaves in the wind, touched everyone's heart, offering comfort and support in times of need.

She was a living embodiment of strength, intelligence, and compassion, a rare and radiant soul in a world that often hungered for such virtues.

She resided with her grandmother, Eudora, who shared stories of the forest's past, of a time when magic flowed freely from its depths. Elara listened with wide-eyed wonder to these tales, yearning to explore the forest's depths herself.

Elara's family, known for their generations-old bakery, had remained in Everwood for as long as anyone could remember. Elara, having a particularly good relationship with much of the townsfolk, was an outcast to many of the children her age. While most of the village children spent their time playing games and having fun, Elara spent most of her time helping her grandmother run the bakery since her parent's disappearance.

One day, as Elara was gazing longingly at the children playing her grandmother told her to go and enjoy the rest of her day. Elated with the idea, Elara kissed her grandmother goodbye and raced to join the children playing near the edge of the forest.

"Hi guys! Can I play with you?" Elara exclaimed.

"Play with us? Like we'd want you ruining our fun," scoffed Helena, one of the older girls in the village.

"Can't you see you aren't welcome here? Your family is cursed," answered Winston, the son of the village leader. "My father told me not to go near you or your crazy grandmother."

Elara looked at Winston confused, "Curse? What do you mean? My family isn't cursed and my grandma isn't crazy!"

"We all know the stories of how your family is the reason the town got cursed," said Helena. The other children looked on and laughed as tears formed in Elara's eyes.

"And as for your Grandmother, I see her rambling to herself all the time, but I guess if I got stuck with you I'd go crazy to," Winston said with a cocky grin on his face.

"I don't know what you're talking about. Why are you guys being so mean?" Tears started to fall down Elara's face when Winston chimed in, "Face it Elara, you don't belong here. Go run back to Grandma, or better yet disappear like your parents."

"I just wanted to play," whimpered Elara as she started to sob, unaware of the vines starting to make their way towards the children.

As the older children were laughing, Eudora looked out the window to see the forest coming alive. She opened the window and shouted for Elara to come home quickly.

Hearing her grandmother's call, Elara raced home crying. Eudora had a sigh of relief as the vines started to recede and the trees went lifeless again.

Eudora asked, "What's wrong child?"

"The kids were laughing at me and saying that our family was cursed and that you were crazy and Winston said I should disappear like Mom and Dad," Elara exclaimed as she hopped into her grandmother's arms sobbing.

"What nonsense! I should march over and speak to their parents this instant," Eudora grumbled as she held Elara tight. "Your parents loved you very much. They would never leave you, they had no other choice."

"Why did they leave grandma?" Elara questioned looking up at Eudora.

"I'll tell you when you're older child. When you're older you'll understand. For now, let's get you some warm milk and a good night's rest," comforted Eudora as she carried Elara to bed.

As Elara drifted off to sleep, Eudora looked out over the forest and sighed. Opening the locket around her neck to gaze at the picture inside of a baby Elara and her mother, "Amelia, what would you do? Her powers are coming forth and I can't show her what she needs to know. It's too soon. She's not ready. I'm not ready."

As night cast its darkening shadow on the house, Eudora laid next to Elara and fell asleep holding her grandchild close.

Since that day on the edge of the forest, as Eudora feared, Elara's powers only continued to grow. Outbursts of raw magic became more common as Elara neared sixteen years of age.

Eudora looked up as Elara charged through the bakery door fuming after another run-in with Winston.

"Should I ask what happened today or are you going to take it out on my cookies again?" Eudora asked as Elara started rolling out the dough.

"I'm fine Grandma. We just have a lot of work to do," exclaimed Elara.

"Was it that boy Winston again?" Eudora asked.

Elara scoffs, "When is it not?"

Eudora chuckled, "I think that boy likes you."

"As if Grandma," exclaimed Elara.

Eudora continued to chuckle as she approached Elara, twirling a strand of Elara's hair around her finger. Eudora continued, "Why not? You're blossoming into a beautiful flower."

"Grandma seriously? Gross," Elara said wrinkling her nose, "He's a troll."

"Mhm, if you say so child," reaching around Elara, Eudora pulls out a slice of chocolate cake, "happy birthday, my little cupcake!" Eudora handed the cake slice to Elara and hugged her tightly.

Elara chuckled, "Thanks Grandma."

"Alright child, what's wrong?" Eudora asked.

Elara met her Grandmother's gaze, "Just wishing Mom and Dad were here to celebrate with us…"

Eudora sighed, "Me too honey," as she walked over and locked the door, "Now then, grab your cake and some milk and let's go upstairs, we have to talk."

Elara asked, "Is everything ok Grandma?"

"Everything's fine, there's just some things you need to know," assured Eudora.

Once settled upstairs with cake and milk, Eudora sighed looking from Elara to the moonlit sky, "You're sixteen now my child and the time has come to tell you what happened to your parents."

Eudora pulled out a small box from her shawl and handed it to Elara, "This was your mother's. I found it on the edge of the forest the day they disappeared."

Opening the box, Elara gasped as a beautiful emerald amulet shone from within, "It's beautiful." A small tear fell from Elara's eye as she wraps the amulet around her neck.

Eudora: "You were so young, you wouldn't remember this. Your parents took you on a picnic in the forest that day. They wanted to show you the wonder and magic within the forest," Eudora kept her gaze out at the night sky as she explained, "You see child, there is a reason the townsfolk think we are cursed. The women of our family come from a long line of emberlyns."

"Grandma, what are you talking about? What's an emberlyn? I don't understand what this has to do with Mom and Dad," asked Elara with a concerned look on her face.

Eudora: "I'm getting there child. Hush up now and pay attention. Each emberlyn controls an element of nature. Your mother controlled the Earth. The forest called to her like I know it does to you."

Elara sat there in silence, she never told her grandmother of the whispers she heard coming from the forest.

"Don't look so shocked child. I've heard the whispers in the wind," Eudora chuckled as she waved her hand and a gust of wind came bursting through the window blowing Elara's hair around her.

Elara: "How did you do that?"

Eudora: "I am an emberlyn of the sky. I can manipulate the air around us. The wind and I even share stories from time to time. It's quite the chatter box too. Always gossiping about something or another. It's also the worlds biggest tattle-tale, even if it does only get half the story right."

Just then a gust of air blew through and swirled around Eudora.

Eudora: "Don't you take that tone with me! It's not MY fault you never fact check before you come talk to me."

After another ruffle through Eudora's shawl, the wind barreled through the window slamming the shutters shut.

Eudora opened the window and called out, "Yeah get out and don't come back until you've changed your attitude!"

Elara: "Grandma?"

Eudora turned to look at Elara, "Yes? What? Oh, where was I dear?"

Elara: "Are we like witches or something?"

Eudora: "Kind of, we don't ride brooms or anything, we are just more in tune with nature. Your mother, like you, felt more empowered and in tune with the Earth. She loved the forest as much as your father did. They shared that passion with you."

Elara: "So Dad was an emberlyn too?"

Eudora: "No child. He was human, mostly anyway. But a lot of the fruits and herbs that are used in his recipes came from the forest. He was going to harvest ingredients as your mother was coming back to town," Eudora laughed, "Your poor father didn't know what hit him. Anyway, stop distracting me. Your parents took you on a picnic that day. I told your mother not to. I told her I heard the rumors of Malachar in the wind. She laughed and said it's fine mother. I warned her not to venture too far into the forest. But she and your father were determined to show you the Heart of the Forest."

Elara: "What's at the Heart of the Forest Grandma?"

Eudora: "Child if you don't hush and let me tell you, you aren't going to know. Now, where was I? Oh yes! They took you with them to the Heart of the Forest and as they were getting ready to settle in the shadows descended. Your mother made a small opening in the tree roots in which to hide you. As your mother placed you inside, the shadows grew and seemed to extinguish all light and color in their path," Eudora took a deep breath before continuing, "Out of the shadows, Malachar appeared."

Elara: "Who is Malachar?"

Eudora: "Malachar is an ancient voodoo shaman. Time had etched a cruel story on his visage, rendering him a haunting figure of desolation. His appearance was a spectral reflection of the evil that dwelled within his heart. With skin ashen and sallow, the shaman's eyes were like dark voids, devoid of any spark of humanity. They seemed to draw you into a bottomless abyss, and their gaze sent shivers down the spine of even the bravest souls. His once-mighty frame had withered to a mere husk, draped in tattered and soiled rags that clung to his emaciated form. Long, twisted strands of grizzled, charcoal hair framed his face, cascading like unkempt vines. The hair had become a tangled, matted mess, echoing the chaos within his soul. It concealed his features as if nature itself sought to shield the world from the malevolent aura that exuded from him. Each step he took seemed to echo with the lamentations of souls whose magic he had devoured. He was a parasitic sorcerer, feeding off the essence of others, leaving them drained and hollow. His skeletal fingers bore talon-like nails, each imbued with the stolen energies of countless victims. His voice was a haunting, raspy whisper carrying the anguish of the souls he had ensnared. The shaman's aura was one of darkness and despair, a living testament to the twisted path he had chosen. His ugliness was not confined to the physical; it emanated from the void where his soul had once resided. He was a wretched specter, feared and reviled by those who knew of his unholy deeds, a true embodiment of the darkness that can consume even the most potent magic."

Elara: "What did he want with Mom and Dad?"

Eudora: "It wasn't that he wanted anything to do with them. He was after something much more powerful. He was after the Guardian of the Forest. Once your parents realized that he intended to capture the Guardian, they tried to stop him. They fought bravely but Malachar was just too powerful. The last of your mother's magic brought you home to me. And that my child, is the whole tale as told by the wind."

Elara stared at her grandmother in awe, "Grandma, that can't be it. Where are they? Where is the Guardian? What happened to Malachar after?"

Eudora: "Elara! One question at a time. Your parents were never found. The Guardian is trapped with Malachar in his land of darkness and shadows. Malachar was wounded. However, wounds heal. He's been regaining his strength and stealing the magic from the Guardian. That's why it's no longer safe to go in the forest. Malachar is sucking the very life force out of the forest and the Guardian to make himself more powerful."

Elara: "So how do we stop him?"

Eudora: "We?! Child, there is no we. WE will do nothing. Did you not hear what I was just saying?"

Elara stared open-mouthed at Eudora, "You told me this for me to do nothing? For me not to avenge my parents? For me to not want to finish what they started? Grandmother, how do you expect me to do nothing?" Elara roared as the Earth shook the house with her rage.

Eudora: "Calm down, calm down, there is still hope. Legend speaks of an emberlyn of great power that will rise and defeat Malachar."

Elara: "Great! Where can we find them?"

Eudora: "Child, if I knew that I would have found them long ago. We will have to be patient. You'll see, when the time is right the Emberlyn will appear and be victorious. Now finish your cake and off to bed with you."

Eudora stood up, kissed Elara, and sent her on her way. Later that night Elara is still awake, looking out the window, *I can't just sit and wait for someone to show up. What if my parents are still out there? Their bodies weren't found so maybe they're trapped. I have so many questions and I'm not going to find them here. I have to go and find them.* Elara rolls out of bed and begins to pack her rucksack. Slipping into trousers and boots she sneaks down to the kitchen to pack some food.

"I knew you wouldn't stay put," Eudora said from the corner, "There's already a satchel of food ready for you." Elara stared stunned as Eudora points to the overfilled satchel of food.

Elara: "Grandmother…you knew…"

Eudora: "Of course I knew child, I did tell you the wind can be a bit of a tattle-tale. Now, The road ahead may be uncertain, but remember that it's the unexpected detours that often lead to the most remarkable discoveries. Embrace the unknown as a friend, not a foe."

Elara grabbed the satchel of food and one last hug. Eudora wrapped a cloak around Elara's shoulders and tucked the amulet into it. Elara kissed Eudora on the cheek and set out towards the looming forest.

As Eudora watched Elara walk off, she whispers into the breeze, "You better keep an eye on her. Do you hear me? If not, so help me I will make a tornado so big nobody will have to worry about Malachar anymore."

The vast forest stretched as far as the eye could see, a sprawling expanse of somber grandeur. It was a realm of shadows and solitude, where the very air seemed heavy with an ancient melancholy. Towering trees, their branches shrouded in dark leaves that barely allowed slivers of sunlight to penetrate, creating a canopy that cast the forest into perpetual twilight.

Beneath the twisted branches, the forest floor was a carpet of decaying leaves, their colors long faded, crunching softly underfoot as if whispering secrets to those who dared to tread there. Many of the trees, long devoid of life, stood as eerie soldiers, their skeletal remains reaching for the heavens in gnarled, skeletal fingers. Their bark was weathered, their trunks hollowed by time, a testament to the ages that had passed.

It was a place where the silence was profound, broken only by the occasional creaking of branches or the faint rustling of leaves. The only signs of life were the resilient fungi and mosses, their muted hues adding a touch of ghostly beauty to the desolation. Even the birds and animals seemed to have abandoned this place, leaving an eerie emptiness that pervaded every corner of the forest.

The air was still, and the atmosphere heavy with a sense of longing, as if the very soul of the forest had been drained away, leaving behind only the remnants of what once thrived. It was a place where time had woven a tapestry of solitude, where the world itself seemed to hold its breath, waiting for something that had long since passed.

As Elara crossed the threshold from the village into the dark forest little did she know that her presence did not go unnoticed, for Malachar sensed an intruder and set his dark plans into motion.

Chapter 2

Elara traveled further into the forest, where the trees loomed tall and ancient, their branches intertwined as if sharing centuries of whispered secrets. She felt both trepidation and fascination as she ventured deeper into the woods.

The forest enveloped her in an eerie silence, broken only by the occasional rustling leaves and the distant calls of unseen creatures. The air was cool and carried a hint of an earthy fragrance. Elara's heart beat a mix of fear and excitement. She couldn't help but wonder about the stories her grandmother had shared.

As Elara followed along a narrow, twisting path, the forest's eerie decay continued to unfold before her. The dim light struggled to penetrate the thick canopy, casting an ominous gloom over the twisted branches and decaying foliage. The path beneath her feet was uneven and covered in damp, rotting leaves. Elara's surroundings revealed a desolate landscape as if nature itself was succumbing to a slow demise.

However, it wasn't just the forest that captivated her; it was a voice, soft and melodious, that seemed to linger in the air. It beckoned her to venture further into the forest, deeper into its heart. The forest was calling to her, and its secrets sang a sweet, alluring melody.

Unbeknownst to Elara high in the treetops, a pair of amber eyes watched her every move. Sylvan, The Gatekeeper, had been drawn to her unique aura. *Strange for a human to come this far, I best make sure she doesn't get lost*, he thought.

He leaped from branch to branch, following Elara as she walked along the path.

"Who are you?" Sylvan exclaimed, high in the trees.

Elara frozen looking around her for the source of the voice.

Elara: "Who…who said that…"

"Up here. What brings you to my forest?" Sylvan inquired.

Startled, Elara looked up to see a giant squirrel with fur as green as emeralds perched on a branch above her.

Elara: "Did you just…talk?"

Sylvan, cocking his head to the side, answered, "Do you see anyone else around here?"

Elara jumped back, tripping on a root, "Oh my…you talk?! What are you? Who are you?"

Sylvan: "I am Sylvan, Gatekeeper of this Forest. I've been watching you. You're unlike the others who have entered our woods."

Elara, looked up from where she fell, "Why are you here?"

Sylvan: "I'm here to guide and protect. There is a dark presence here who has cast a shadow over the forest. Now I shall ask you again what brings you to my forest?"

Elara looked at Sylvan, deciding to be cautious in her response, "I'm…I'm exploring the forest. I wanted to see for myself if the rumors were true."

Sylvan, his bushy-tail twitched, "If the rumors are true huh? If you're going to lie, at least make it believable. Want to try again?"

Elara: "I am just exploring!"

Sylvan: "Let's try this again. What's your name and why have you come here?"

Recognizing that Sylvan possessed a discerning insight that would easily pierce through any lie, Elara decided to reveal the truth.

Elara: "My name is Elara, and I have come to find out what happened to my parents."

Sylvan: "You're parents?"

Elara: "My parents disappeared 15 years ago; my grandmother told me they were last seen in these woods."

Sylvan: "Elara I am sorry to hear about your parents, but nothing could survive in these woods for that long in its current state. However, if you're determined to explore, I'll be your guide, but you must promise to listen and stay close."

Elara: "I'm ok, I'm sure you have much more important things to do than following me."

Sylvan: "Quite the contrary, My day is completely open, and I insist the forest can be dangerous for someone that doesn't know their way around."

Elara hesitant, "If you insist."

Sylvan: "So do we have a deal? I will help you as long as you promise to listen and stay close."

Elara: "I promise."

Sylvan's eyes glittered with approval as he leaped down from the branch to join her.

Sylvan: "Then come, young one. Our journey is just beginning."

Elara's footsteps became more sure as she followed Sylvan deeper into the forest. As they ventured further, the forest's beauty unfolded before her like pages from a magical book.

The dappled sunlight played on the leaves, casting dancing shadows and illuminating the vibrant colors of exotic flowers.

Elara: "I've never seen anything so beautiful. "

Sylvan, her newfound guide and friend, smiled: "You're getting closer to the Heart of the Forest. It is one of the places that Malachar's magic has not touched. You'll find many flora and creatures flourish within the Heart."

Elara: "This is amazing…it feels like home…"

Sylvan: "This forest was once a place of pure enchantment, where magic flowed freely, and Borealis' radiance could be seen every day. The villagers and the creatures of the forest lived in harmony. But Malachar, with his greed for power, sought to control it all, casting this dark spell over it."

Elara: "Who is Borealis?"

Sylvan: "WHAT? You do not know of the Guardian of the Forest? Borealis is only the most powerful being to ever set foot in this realm! He is a shape-shifting God of Nature, weaving his magic to nurture the land and make it bountiful. In his truest form, he appears as a majestic stag with antlers adorned in vines and leaves, a symbol of the forest's vitality. At times, he transforms into a colossal butterfly, its wings painted with the hues of the sunrise, fluttering gracefully as the embodiment of nature's delicate balance. The mere sight of him, whether in the form of a stag or a butterfly, invoke awe and reverence among all creatures lucky enough to witness his presence."

Elara: "What happened to him?"

Sylvan: "Borealis was captured by Malachar."

Elara: "What did Malachar want with Borealis?"

Sylvan: "His power of course, one of the unique gifts of Borealis is to bring life, soul, and peace where needed. Malachar spent years in search of Borealis in hopes of capturing him and using his magic to retrieve his soul and take control of the forest."

Elara: "What happened to his soul?"

Sylvan paused, causing Elara to stop beside him.

Sylvan: "Unlike white magic that brings light, such as the likes of Borealis, white witches, and emberlyns, dark magic takes and the more you conjure the more life it takes, eventually leaving you a soulless husk that drains the life out of everything around you."

Elara: "So how did Malachar capture Borealis?"

Sylvan: "Long ago my good friend, Amelia, the Champion of the Forest, was presenting her child to Borealis for his blessing to make her the next Champion. Amelia was an emberlyn. She helped keep order and prosperity in the forest."

Sylvan, took a deep breath, centering himself before continuing, "Borealis was distracted when the shadows descended encasing everything in darkness. Amelia and I tried to defend our Guardian but to no avail. You see, Malachar used the shadows to distract Borealis and Amelia so he could capture the child. Using his shaman staff, Malachar was able to capture the soul of the child, and would only release her if Borealis would take the child's place. Agreeing to this, Borealis switched places with Amelia's child. Amelia and her husband fought valiantly, but Malachar with the power of the Guardian triumphed and sent them to the shadow realm."

Elara: "And what happened to the child."

Sylvan, looking forlorn, "Nobody knows, I've spent years searching for her. There are rumors she was banished to the shadow realm with her parents, and some say that her mother used the last bit of her magic to save her."

Elara: "What do you believe? How did you escape?"

Sylvan: "I believe the little one is still alive. I feel it in my bones that she is. As for how I escaped…well, I was knocked out by Malachar's demons trying to save the child. When I came to, I raced back to the battle, only to find my friends being taken by shadows and Borealis captured. I couldn't help them anymore, and someone had to guard the Heart of the Forest."

Elara, holding back tears as she found out the truth of what happened to her parents, listened intently, her eyes filled with a mixture of sadness and determination.

The stories of the forest's past, with it's lost magic and the imprisoned guardian, stirred a deep desire to make things right.

Elara: "I want to help. I want to free the forest from Malachar's grip and bring back the magic."

Sylvan nodded, his bushy tail twitching, "Your courage is admirable, Elara. But the journey would be perilous. The forest has become treacherous under Malachar's influence and must be tread carefully. I can not as Gatekeeper allow you, a human, to risk your life for such foolish notions."

Elara smirked, "Well lucky for you I'm not human, I'm an emberlyn."

Sylvan rolled his eyes, "Elara, we don't have time to play games, I will help you search for any signs of your parents once that is complete I will escort you back to Everwood."

Elara: "Sylvan you don't understand I really am!"

Sylvan scoffed, "I thought we were passed lying to each other. I am done with this nonsense first thing tomorrow I will escort you back to Everwood."

Elara: "I'M NOT LYING!"

Sylvan stared at her with an arrogant smirk and smiled.

"Fine, I'll show you," Elara raised her arms, closed her eyes, and tried to get the vines to move only to hear Sylvan's laughter. In her mind, she was taken back to Everwood being laughed at by Winston and Helena.

Sylvan continued chuckling as the ground from under him fell away. Sylvan began to fall down the hole, as a vine grabs his tail, pulling him back up and throwing him in the brook.

Sylvan came out of the water to scold Elara.

Elara, frantic, rushed to help him, "Sylvan I'm so sorry. I didn't know that was going to happen!"

Sylvan, shaking the water out of his fur, sputtered, "You're going to need to work on your control. Especially if we're going to be taking on Malachar."

Elara, shocked and elated: "SO I CAN COME?"

Sylvan: "As long as you promise not to squirrel-handle me again."

Elara chuckled, "I'll try, but I can't make any promises."

As they continued, Sylvan shared his wisdom about the hidden paths of the forest and the ways to navigate its enchantments. Elara marveled at the wonders that surrounded her.

The iridescent butterflies, the whispering leaves, and the ancient trees all spoke to her in their own way, welcoming her into their world.

The forest's enchanting call grew stronger, its magic humming in the air like a timeless melody. Sylvan taught Elara to listen to the whispers of the leaves, to understand the language of the wind, and to appreciate the quiet beauty that thrived in this magical realm.

As the days turned to night, they found themselves near a serene brook, its waters shimmering like liquid crystal under the fading sunlight. Elara knelt by the brook, captivated by its tranquility, her reflection dancing in the clear waters.

Sylvan joined her and perched on a moss-covered rock, his amber eyes glistening.

Sylvan: "This is a place of magic, Elara. Our journey has only just begun, and there are more secrets to uncover and challenges to face. But remember, the forest will protect those who respect it."

As the stars began to twinkle in the night sky, Elara couldn't help but think about her grandmother. *Grandmother said that the wind spoke to her. Maybe I can let her know that I'm alright and I've met Sylvan,* Elara thought.

Elara whispered, "Grandma, I'm ok. I've begun the journey to defeat Malachar. I've met the Gatekeeper, Sylvan. He's going to help. I hope you are alright. I love you."

Sylvan: "Talking to the wind young one?"

Elara: "Yeah. Hoping that it will carry my message back to my grandmother."

Sylvan patted Elara on the shoulder, "It will. The wind may be tricky but the messages get through. At least it's what Amelia used to tell me. Try and get some sleep Elara. We have a big day tomorrow."

Elara: "What's tomorrow?"

Sylvan: "Your first day of training."

Chapter 3

THUD! Elara woke up to a fish flopping next to her head. She leaped from the ground, shrieking as she looked over and saw Sylvan stretching.

Sylvan: "Rise and shine, it's time to get started."

Elara: "What's with the fish?"

Sylvan: "It's breakfast, and full of protein."

Elara: "I'm not touching that thing."

Sylvan: "Have you never had fish before?"

Elara: "No I've had fish, just not alive and flopping next to me."

Sylvan: "I'll prepare breakfast while you stretch."

Elara gave Sylvan a look making him pause. He'd seen that look before. *But it couldn't be..could it?* He thought. Shaking his head, as if to clear it.

Elara watched as Sylvan showed her how to properly prepare and cook the fish. As they ate, Sylvan heard a rustling in the trees.

Elara: "Sylvan what…."

Sylvan: "Shush. Stay here."

Sylvan dashed toward the bushes where the noise came from and pounced on an unsuspecting guest.

Out from the bushes came a massive blue raccoon. The raccoon was grumbling to himself rubbing where Sylvan had pounced.

Sylvan emerged from the bushes, "Rascal. I should have known it was you following us."

Rascal sarcastically greeted Sylvan, "Well well well, what have we here? A human? I know you missed me Sylvan, but what a dull substitution."

Elara couldn't help but smile at the raccoon's cheeky demeanor.

Sylvan sighed, "Be gone Rascal, we have no need for your antics here."

Rascal: "No need to get all squirrelly. I just couldn't resist the allure of an adventure. You know me, I do enjoy stirring the pot."

Rascal, turned to face Elara, "My name's Rascal, Sylvan's best friend, and the only one that still likes to have a good time in this place."

Sylvan rolled his eyes, before busying himself with cleaning up what remained of breakfast.

Rascal, stage whispered to Elara, "He likes to pretend he hates me because I remind him that he used to be fun."

Sylvan grumbled, "Some of us had to grow up and take responsibility."

Rascal, sighed dramatically, "I know the story Mr. Gatekeeper."

Elara, tried not to laugh, extending her hand to introduce herself, "I'm Elara, and I've always been fascinated by the forest. Sylvan is showing me around."

Rascal's eyes gleamed with interest. He was intrigued by Elara's comment. Knowing what lay ahead he couldn't help but press further.

Rascal: "Surely, Sylvan wouldn't be leading you this way. This path leads to Malachar's lair. You should be taking this young maiden to Amelia's Garden or Erik's Hollow. They are much nicer and far more beautiful than what lies ahead."

Sylvan: "We are getting ready to begin Elara's training session. So if you'll excuse us."

Rascal: "Training huh? Whatcha training for?"

Sylvan, glared at Rascal, "That doesn't concern you now off you go."

Rascal, threw his paws up, "Alright alright, I know when I'm not wanted. Don't get your tail in a twist."

Elara: "It was nice meeting you."

Rascal, his eyes sparkled with mischief, "We'll be seeing each other real soon."

Rascal disappeared into the underbrush and out of sight.

Sylvan scoffed, "Now that he's out of our fur. Let us begin."

Sylvan: "Alright Elara, please sit down and cross your legs. Yes, that's it. Now take a deep breath in and let it out slowly. Once your mind and body have relaxed your Chakra will be able to flow easier making your powers more manageable. You see, as an emberlyn you are more in tune with the vibrations and life force of the world around you. I want you to empty your mind and just listen to the sounds of the Earth. I want you to put your hands on the ground and feel the vibrations of the animals."

Elara ran her fingers through the grass, her fingers getting moist with morning dew, "Nothing's happening."

Sylvan: "Focus, now as an emberlyn your body already knows what to do, it's instinctual. It's not like a witch who has to cast a spell or brew a potion. Your powers are an extension of you, that's why when you get emotional your powers surface. What we are going to do is focus your magic so that it flows out of you effortlessly. Now I want you to tell me how many worms are under the rock next to you."

Elara: "I can't do that."

Sylvan: "Yes you can, but it will only work if you believe you can. As an Earth Emberlyn, you have special connections with the Earth, and if you focus not only can you feel the rock, but any vibrations coming from the rock."

Elara, this time she dug her fingers into the dirt, "I can't feel anything"

Sylvan: "YES YOU CAN."

Elara: "But I….."

Sylvan: "YES YOU CAN NOW TELL ME HOW MANY WORMS ARE UNDER THAT ROCK."

Elara: "Uh…SIX."

Sylvan picked up the rock, "One, two, three, four, five, six….See I told you that you could do it."

Elara jumped up and hugged Sylvan, "I DID IT I CAN'T BELIEVE IT!"

Sylvan smiled, patting Elara on her back, "Not bad, we will

continue more training later, for now, let us get moving, Borealis only knows where that bushy-tailed raccoon is."

Elara: "You know if we keep making progress like this we'll be able to stop Malachar in no time."

Rascal's voice came from the bushes, "Malachar, huh? That's a name that gives us all the heebie-jeebies. You know, I've been lurking in these woods for quite some time, and I've seen a thing or two. I might have some tricks up my furry sleeve that could help you."

Sylvan: "Yes, you do a lot of lurking about. Especially where you are unwanted. Get out of the bushes!"

Elara, moved towards Rascal, as he emerged from the bushes, "We're here to bring back the magic and free the Guardian. If you're willing to help, Rascal, we'd be grateful."

Sylvan remained skeptical, as Rascal's reputation for mischief was well known. But Elara sensed an opportunity to gain a new ally.

Rascal's eyes twinkled with mischief as he considered the offer.

Rascal: "Alrighty then you've got yourself a raccoon. I'll show you the ropes and some hidden tricks only a forest dweller like me knows."

Sylvan: "If you are to join us Rascal there will be no tricks or mischief. I mean it so help me I will smite you where you stand should you even think of…"

Rascal turned to face Sylvan while showing Elara his crossed fingers, "Yes yes yes oh mighty Gatekeeper. We shall have a boring, no-nonsense journey for the fear you'll singe my fur with that look on your face."

Rascal winked at Elara as Sylvan launched into a lecture on the responsibility of duty and honor on such a perilous journey. Elara couldn't help but chuckle softly as Rascal and Sylvan continued to bicker back and forth as they began to make their way deeper into the forest.

Elara: "You two bicker like an old married couple."

Rascal: "Old yes. Couple never. Sylvan is too much of a stickler for the rules for me. I have standards."

Sylvan grumbled, "Standards?! The only standards you have, you ruffian, are from yesterday's scraps. You wouldn't know standards if they bit off your tail."

Rascal: "I'll leave the biting to you, old friend. You and your buck teeth."

Elara felt a sense of camaraderie as the trio descended deeper into the forest. However, not far away, Nightshade, a tiny, malnourished, purple bat with fragile, tattered wings and yellow beady eyes that perpetually shimmered with fear and anxiety, was frantically looking for the Gatekeeper.

Nightshade: "Where oh where is that blasted Gatekeeper? I knew I shouldn't have stopped for that gooseberry bush. How hard is it to keep watch over a squirrel? Oh Master will have my head on a stick for this. 'Keep watch Nightshade. You must never let him out of your sight'. Oh, I'm going to be a roasted, toasted batcicle."

Elara: "Alright boys enough fighting. We have work to do!"

Rascal: "Then follow me, my dear lady."

Sylvan: "Rascal not that way. That's towards the marshes. WE need to go to the right to Hollows."

Nightshade turned his head as he flew over the trio, "Whoa What?!" SMACK! THUD! CRASH! "Ow! Brilliant Nightshade, just brilliant. You're stuck in a tree. What would Master say if he could see you now?"

After freeing himself, Nightshade shook off the sap from his wings and looked around for the trio only to find that they had gone.

Nightshade: "Oh Master isn't going to like this one bit. He's going to add me to a batch of boiled bat stew when I tell him."

Nightshade took to the skies flying every which way but straight. His tiny heart beating as frantically as his wings.

Chapter 4

Sylvan, wiped his paws, before placing them on his hips, " Now Elara, focus on moving the rock. No, not that one. The smaller one, yes, good. Focus on where you want it to go. For example, you can throw it at Rascal."

Rascal, placed a paw on his chest, with a faux offended look on his face, "Why do I have to be target practice? Why can't you be target practice and I teach?"

Sylvan, turned his back to Rascal, "Because you've never taught a day in your life. Much less teaching an emberlyn how to correctly use her powers. Now hush and let me work."

Rascal sputtered, "Neither have you!"

Sylvan scoffed, "No, but I have done extensive research on the topic."

Elara chuckled at the antics of her companions before taking a deep breath and cleared her mind of everything except moving the rock.

Sylvan smiled as the rock rolled towards him.

Sylvan, clapped his paws, "Well done Elara! Well done indeed!"

Elara, slumped, disappointed, "I wanted it to float, not roll."

Sylvan: "Ah yes. But the task was for you to move the rock. Rolling is still moving. Which is what we will do. Move forward with the next step. Now I want you to focus on moving the vines on the trees."

Elara said in a dejected tone, "I'm not sure I'm ready for that Sylvan. I can barely move a rock."

Rascal called from his lounging spot on the log, "Elara, you can do whatever you put your mind to. You came into your powers basically yesterday, it's only been a few days AND you're already moving the rocks. Might as well try the vines. Think of it as a dance. Just three easy steps. 1. Breathe. 2. Focus. 3. Power! It's that simple. Don't let the old windbag tell you differently."

Sylvan sighed in aggravation, "Are you quite finished? You'll only confuse the poor thing. Elara, just believe in your abilities, as I do. You can do this. Feel your magic and give it a try."

Elara looked from Sylvan to the vines before closing her eyes.

Sylvan: "Now feel the world around you and manipulate it to your will."

Elara could see the vines hanging lifeless and dull against the gnarled branches of the long-dead tree. She could see the vines becoming lush and green again and beginning to weave and twist through the tree as flowers sprouted from them. She imagined them moving as if weaving a blanket of color in the otherwise bleak world.

Sylvan softly murmured, "Elara, open your eyes."

Upon opening her eyes, much to her shock, Elara saw the vines doing exactly what she imagined them doing. Before her and her companions, the tree and vines had come to life. Bursting forth with rich hues of green as the vines wined their way in and out of the hallowed tree.

Sylvan: "You did it. You did it Elara."

Elara embraced Sylvan tightly and whispered, "Thank you for believing in me."

Rascal, munched on an apple and shouted, "I believed in you too."

Sylvan rubbing his face tiredly, whined, "Must you always have something to say?"

Rascal with a cheeky grin, "I'm so glad you've noticed."

Elara: "What's the next step Sylvan?"

Sylvan looked at the Sun setting, "The next step is getting a good night's rest after a well-deserved meal. How about you make yourself useful, for once, Rascal, and catch some fish or find some berries for dinner eh?"

Rascal opened one eye from his perch on the log, "I guess if I must."

Sylvan crossed his arms and raised an eyebrow, "You must..."

Rascal finished his apple and tossed the core aside, "Fine. Fine. One banquet coming right up."

As Rascal went off in search of food, Elara looked to Sylvan.

Sylvan: "Care to share what's on your mind Elara?"

Sylvan lead Elara to the abandoned log to sit.

Elara: "I don't know what you mean Sylvan. I'm just ready to begin the next part of my training."

Sylvan: "You seem to be elsewhere."

A light breeze blew through the trees, ruffling Elara's hair. *Trust the Gatekeeper, he will not lead you astray.* Elara's eyes widen as she hears her grandmother's whispered message before turning to look at Sylvan.

Elara: "I guess I'm thinking of my parents. I want to know what happened to them. I also am thinking about what comes next for my training. I'm also worried about the challenges that we face on the road ahead. I don't know Sylvan. What if I'm not ready by the time we face Malachar?"

Sylvan looked at Elara's worried features, and took her hand in his paw, "The path to greatness is paved with audacity, not certainty. Embrace the unknown, for therein lies the magic of true potential."

Rascal walked back into camp, "Enough with this wishy-washy stuff. It's time to chow down!"

Dropping his catch of the day, which consisted of an assortment of berries, a few fish, and various nuts; Rascal looked at Sylvan and Elara and grinned broadly.

Sylvan: "I'm almost impressed."

Rascal bumped Sylvan with his shoulder as he gathered wood to start a fire, "You ARE impressed you whiskered old coot. Just admit it."

Sylvan laughed, "Alright. I'm impressed you did well Rascal."

Rascal: "Now was that so hard? Haha. Let's eat up and get a good night's sleep. We should be at the Grove tomorrow, wouldn't you say Sylvan?"

Elara looked between the two forest dwellers, "The Grove? What grove?"

Sylvan smiled softly, "It is a place of indescribable beauty, the very air is imbued with magic. As you enter the Grove, you are immediately enveloped by the vibrant colors and sweet scents of the lush flora that surrounds you. Gigantic, ancient trees with moss-covered bark tower overhead. As you make your way towards the heart of the grove, the sound of water begins to grow more pronounced. At its center lies a magnificent, crystalline waterfall, where the memories of those who have visited before are said to be preserved. The water cascades from a rocky ledge, forming a curtain of liquid crystals that shimmers with an otherworldly radiance. Rainbows dance in the spray, creating a mesmerizing display of colors that seem to come to life."

Rascal, interrupted, "If you keep talking you're gonna ruin the Grove for her. Let her be surprised tomorrow."

Across the forest, Nightshade was making his way to Malachar's lair.

Panting heavily, his wings gave out from exhaustion, Nightshade fell at the feet of the coyote, Bayonne. A foulsome creature with fangs yellowed by neglect, mangy knotted fur adorned his lethal body. His body was malnourished and littered with scars of battles long past. Bayonne's soulless black eyes narrow as they take in the tiny bat.

Bayonne snarled, "Well look what the bat dragged in?" Stomping his foot down, Nightshade barely managed to avoid his massive paw, "You heard Malachar. Your duty is to watch that good-for-nothing squirrel."

Nightshade panted, "That's what I need to tell Master. The Gatekeeper is on the move. He's with a raccoon…"

Bayonne interrupted, "So he's got himself a playmate. What of it bat?"

Nightshade wobbled around in an attempt to get to his feet, "He's got a human with him. They're on the…" SPLAT! Bayonne's paw pushes Nightshade back to the ground.

Bayonne: "You've been drinking too much nectar. No human would dare enter here. Come off it."

Nightshade tried and failed to get himself out from under the massive paw.

Nightshade muffled, "I saw them Bayonne. They're on the path heading this way! We must tell Master!"

Bayonne chuckled and scoffed, "Even if it were true, they won't make it past…"

Malachar: "Now Bayonne, what did I tell you about playing with your food?"

Bayonne and Nightshade both glared towards the entrance of the cave. The light from the torches get covered by darkness, fog covered the floor, and a smell of rot and decay began to take over the cave. Malachar exclaimed, "Why have you returned?"

Nightshade: "Well sire, it might be easier for me to explain if I didn't have this flea-infested mutt on me."

Malachar walked up the steps to his seat, waved his finger, gray fog came from the tip and spiraled towards Bayonne. WHAM! Bayonne got thrown into the side of the cave.

Bayonne: "Why I oughta!"

Malachar: "You oughta what, you mangy mutt." Malachar's shadows grabbed Bayonne by the neck and brought him over to Malachar, his hind paws, barely tall enough to touch the ground to offer a sigh of relief. "Do I need to remind you of your place? You work for me, you live for me, I own you, the only reason you live is because I will it."

Malachar released his grip from Bayonne. Bayonne fell to the floor, picked himself up, and walked away.

Malachar: "Now speak bat."

Nightshade flew over to Malachar, "Well sire, I mean your malevolence, your lordship"

Malachar: "Get on with it!"

Nightshade: "Yes master of course! I was flying, watching the squirrel, just like you wanted. I got very hungry so I went and found a gooseberry bush to munch on. I didn't think anything of it since the squirrel never leaves his tree. Day in and day out he gets up, does a walk about the roots, and goes back into his nest........"

Malachar grabbed Nightshade and held him upside down over a boiling pot of stew, "Do you like the smell of this stew Nightshade."

Nightshade took a deep whiff of the stew, "Oh yes Master, it smells delightful, yes it does Master, what kind of stew is it."

Malachar: "Boiled Bat Stew, and do you know what ingredient is missing."

Malachar started to lower Nightshade closer and closer to the cauldron, "OH NO MASTER! I AM SORRY, I AM SORRY!" Nightshade shook as he held onto Malachar's finger for dear life.

Malachar: "Then get to it! What have you seen." He continued to lower Nightshade into the cauldron. Picking off Nightshade's hold of his finger, "One piggy, two piggies," holding on with one last paw Nightshade exclaimed, "A HUMAN! THEY HAVE A HUMAN!" Malachar throws Nightshade down, the cauldron disappearing in a sea of smog. Nightshade fell on the floor, he covered his eyes with his wings, in the middle of the floor, shaking.

He opened one eye to see Malachar looking at him. Malachar gave him a crooked smile, "Go on."

Nightshade took a sigh of relief and struggled to his feet. Keeping his eyes downcast, "The Gatekeeper is accompanied by two others Master. He has a raccoon and a human girl with him. They are nearing the Grove if they've not already made it there. They were at the brook when I smashed into the tree."

Nightshade shook with fear as the silence became deafening, "I didn't get to hear much of what they were saying but they are making their way towards us… Master they're coming to destroy you."

Malachar smiled a twisted, evil smile.

Nightshade: "Master, are you ok?"

Malachar laughed a dark, and sinister laugh, "Sooooo that little bushy-tailed cockroach wants more? Huh? And a human, they recruited a human. Something's not adding up." Malachar paced back and forth, holding his fingers to his chin as he thought. "I knew I sensed something come into the forest. But what harm could she do, and as for that pipsqueak he couldn't even save his Guardian, let alone his friend, when push came to shove, he ran." Malachar looked into the jewel on top of his staff. A crystal ball, filled with smog, so dark you could barely see the butterfly concealed inside. "Don't worry Barry, I will make sure your friends never see the light of day this time." Malachar kissed his jewel and called for Nightshade.

Malachar: "Don't worry they won't live to see another day."

Nightshade smiled and flew next to Malachar, "What are you going to do Master."

Malachar: "Something I should have done to that pesky squirrel long ago."

Malachar slammed down the bottom of his staff. His eyes glowed green as fog and smoke began to pour out of his mouth while souls and demons flew out and surrounded the cave.

Malachar shouted, "Cursed brethren, the time has come. We emerge from the shadows, united by common darkness. Our way of life has become threatened. The opposition in their deluded hope, underestimate our might. But today, they shall know the full depth of their folly. The hour of reckoning is upon us. March forth, and let the world tremble at thy might. Find the Gatekeeper, and destroy him and his friends. Let nothing get in the way. Do this and all of the souls in the forest will be yours."

The group of demons turn into wolves, while the group of souls turn into foxes, and stormed out of the cave.

Chapter 5

"Keep up slow pokes. It's just up the way," Sylvan exclaimed as he hopped from tree to tree above Elara and Rascal's heads.

Elara, glared up at Sylvan, panting from exhaustion, "Are we almost there? We've been walking all morning."

Rascal lounged on the tail of Elara's cloak, eating the berries left from breakfast, "I don't know what you're going on about Elara, it's a glorious morning."

Elara yanked on her cloak, sending Rascal tumbling on the forest floor.

Elara sighed, "Ah much better…."

Rascal picked himself off the floor and grunts, "For you maybe."

Sylvan dropped down in front of the pair and asked, "What's taking you two so long? The Grove is just ahead."

Elara looked skeptical, "You've said that hours ago too. Are you sure we're going in the right direction?"

Rascal laughed at the offended look on Sylvan's face, "Hahaha! She got you Sylvan! Oh that's spectacular!"

Sylvan scoffed, "If you don't believe me then he can lead you. I'll meet you two there," with a swish of his bushy tail, Sylvan shot off into the treetops disappearing into the leaves.

Elara: "I didn't mean to offend him…"

Rascal: "Oh you didn't. Believe me, it takes more than that to offend that smelly old squirrel. He thinks we can't find the Grove without him and all his 'wisdom'. Ha! We'll show him. Follow me Elara, I'll get us there."

Rascal flicked his tail as he took the lead. Elara adjusted her cloak tighter, keeping an eye out for Sylvan.

Rascal panted, "The Grove is a wondrous place, Elara. It doesn't look like much at first but once you enter the cave everything will be different. You'll see. It's just through here…TADA!"

Rascal jumped and extended his arms towards the cave entrance.

Elara looked skeptical, "Rascal, it's just a cave."

Rascal turned to peer into the cave and Scratched his head. He entered the cave, mumbling to himself, "There has to be a switch or button. Maybe there's a rune?" Running his paws over the wall of the cave, Rascal continued to grumble to himself.

Elara: "Should we, maybe, find Sylvan?"

Rascal: "No no! Just watch!"

Rascal backed up to where Elara stood, then took a running leap into the entrance of the cave, only to fall to the floor with a resounding THUD.

Elara: "Rascal! Are you ok?!"

Out of the darkness came an all too familiar voice, "Are you quite done causing a ruckus?" Seeming to materialize out of thin air appeared Sylvan with a smug look on his furry face.

Rascal grumbled, "I told you I knew the way."

Looking up at Sylvan, Rascal gave a small smirk and raised his paw, "Well don't just stand there gawking."

Sylvan: "If I didn't know you as well as I do, I'd be tempted to help. But because I know you as well as I do, my answer is...no."

Stepping over the sprawled raccoon, Sylvan moved towards Elara who has been taking in the massive expanse of darkness that the cave provided.

Sylvan: "Elara, would you like to enter the Grove now?"

Rascal, picked himself up off the ground, "No she came all this way just for a dark cave. It's glorious ain't it kid, alright let's go home."

Elara followed Sylvan back to the entrance of the cave where Rascal was dusting himself off.

Rascal: "We did this part already."

Sylvan: "Closed minds are like locked doors, unable to perceive the beauty and opportunities that lie just beyond."

Rascal mumbled to Elara, "What's that supposed to mean?"

Sylvan: "Allow me to show you."

Sylvan took a deep breath and closed his eyes, his arms laid flat on each side. The forest grew silent, and the wind grew quiet, as the trees turned deafeningly still.

As Sylvan stood within the entrance of the cave, the very essence of nature itself seemed to respond to his presence. His entire being radiated with a resplendent emerald green as if he were an embodiment of the forest's life force. With each passing moment, the gentle caress of the wind around him transformed into a symphony of whispered secrets, rustling leaves, and the soft, harmonious breath of the trees.

The flowers, in awe of Sylvan's presence, burst forth in a riot of colors, their petals unfurling like a thousand silent applause. They spiraled around him in a mesmerizing dance, painting the air with vivid shades of crimson, sapphire, and gold. Their fragrance, an intoxicating perfume, lingered, weaving dreams in the minds of all who were fortunate enough to witness this magical moment.

Sylvan's eyes, as he slowly opened them, shimmered with the brilliance of molten gold. As they met the cave's entrance, they unleashed radiant beams of light, like the Sun breaking through the dense forest canopy. The cave itself seemed to respond to his gaze, the rocks and walls glowed as if revealing long-lost secrets hidden in their depths.

With a graceful movement, Sylvan lifted his hand to his heart, and then with determination, he pointed toward the cave's entrance. As his fingertips directed their energy, water began to pour forth from the stone, cascading over the cave's mouth like a shimmering curtain. The water flowed with such elegance and power, creating a majestic waterfall that not only concealed the Grove from onlookers but also embodied the profound connection between Sylvan and the sacred sanctuary that now enveloped him.

Elara stared in awe, as Rascal let out, "Where did that come from?!"

Sylvan smiled smugly, "And you thought Gatekeeper was just a title."

Sylvan took Elara's hand and pulled her through the water, "Welcome to the Hidden Grove."

Rascal jumped through the water, "He put so much work in the place, you'd think he'd take the time to give it a name."

Elara's eyes lit up as if seeing nature for the first time.

Elara: "What.. how.. who?"

Sylvan: "Borealis, of course!"

Elara: "Sylvan, what is this place?"

Sylvan's tail twitched with a mixture of sadness and determination.

Sylvan: "This is the Hidden Grove, a place of memories. Here, you may find answers about your parents and how to save Borealis. The Grove holds the echoes of those who visited before. Close your eyes, take a deep breath and let the Grove be your guide."

Elara closed her eyes and inhaled deeply, feeling a connection to the spirits of the Grove. She opened her eyes as images began to flicker before her, like spectral memories taking form against the flowing waterfall cascading from the cave's wall.

She saw her parents, young and full of life, on a fateful picnic in the forest. They laughed and basked in the magic that once flowed freely. She watched as her mother sat in a patch of sunlight by a small puddle where a baby Elara started kicking her feet in. Her mother's laughter was like that of tinkling bells and her smile was as blinding as the Sun they basked in as she smiled at Sylvan saying, "Sylvan, my dear friend, come meet my little one, Elara."

Elara watched as a young Sylvan looked down at her in her mother's arms. Sylvan's smile was wide as he playfully splashed Elara and chuckled at Elara's little squeal.

Sylvan: "So this will be our new Champion? She's a little too small for such a big responsibility Amelia."

Sylvan grinned at Amelia and jumped away from the splash that she sent his way.

Amelia, with her green eyes sparkling, "Oh Sylvan, like the trees, she'll grow. We'll teach her the ways of the forest. She'll grow to respect this sacred place. She'll add to the light." She smiled down at the splashing Elara.

Elara continued to watch the memory unfold as it refocused on Elara's father and Borealis.

Elara's father, Erik, stood tall and proud before Borealis in his butterfly form. Erik's salt and pepper hair and beard were a striking contrast to her mother's bright auburn hair. His piercing blue eyes looked like they could penetrate like the icicles they resembled. Not overly muscular but lethal and scarred.

Erik: "Borealis, you should hide. Take precautions and take cover. The whispers are becoming a roar. Malachar is on the move. I'm telling you, Borealis. He's coming for you." Elara listened to her father's dark timber of a voice.

Borealis: "In the eternal battle between light and darkness, goodness, kindness, and love are the radiant forces that conquer the shadows of evil, hatred, and darkness.

Erik: "But…"

Borealis, placed a comforting foreleg on Erik's shoulder, "Erik, I understand your concern, however Malachar is too weak to come here. You and Amelia made sure of that."

Erik looked lovingly over to where Amelia and Elara were playing, "We had to make sure this place was safe for her. Please consider what I said. You mean so much to all the forest and Amelia."

Borealis: "I will heed your warning. I know he is out there. However, here in the Heart, we are safe. Now, let me meet my new Champion."

Amelia beamed as Borealis and Erik walked over.

Erik smiled at his wife before joining her on the forest floor.

Amelia: "Borealis, allow me the honor of introducing you to our newest little dew drop, Elara." A bunch of leaves swoop under Elara and raised her to Borealis' face. Elara grabbed one of Borealis' antennae and began to chew on it.

Borealis squinted in pain, "She will do nicely." Borealis placed his head on Elara's, "Child of the Forest, I bless you with purity and protection. Let your heart stay as pure as the morning dew, and a shield against darkness. As you walk through these enchanted woods, may you shield the sanctity of this realm. Carry this blessing within you, and be a guardian of the forest's magic."

Suddenly, darkness and shadows surrounded them. Fog appeared, the forest began to fade, and the smell of rot ensued. The shadows pulled Amelia and Erik away from the Guardian.

Borealis handed Elara to Sylvan, "Take her to the Grove and seal it shut!" Sylvan with Elara wrapped in his tail took off running.

Malachar appeared, his voice dripping with a sinister yet desperate tone, and confronted Borealis, "Ah, Borealis, you arrogant fool. It seems fate has finally brought us together. I must admit, I've been hunting you down for quite some time."

Borealis, radiant and resolute, regarded Malachar with a mixture of caution.

Borealis: "Your pursuit has not gone unnoticed, Malachar. But what is it that you seek from me?"

Malachar: "As it turns out the one side effect of my power is that it has left me drained, and my soul desolate. The very essence of my existence has withered."

Borealis, with a glimmer of compassion, replied, "The path

you've chosen has led you to this abyss, Malachar. What do you expect from me?"

Malachar: "I visited the Moirai who told me of a way to heal myself. To fill the void within, I must harness the power of your light. They said that by embracing your power, I could gain mastery over both the white and the dark magic that course through my veins."

The argument between Borealis and Malachar had escalated into a fierce battle of words, each one accusing the other of selfish intent. The forest seemed to hold its breath, aware of the imminent eruption of darkness.

Amelia, her hands trembling with Earth magic, raised a protective barrier to fend off the encroaching shadows. Her husband, Erik, fought valiantly with a makeshift weapon, defending her as they struggled to hold their ground.

Amelia: "We have to protect Elara, Erik! Keep those shadows at bay!"

Erik: "I'll do what I can, Amelia. Just stay behind the barrier!"

Sylvan, baby Elara wrapped in the protective coils of his emerald tail, swung gracefully from the trees, his eyes darting around for any sign of danger. But the moment Elara stirred, his heart leaped, and he momentarily lost focus.

Sylvan: "Hush, little one, stay still… I've got you."

But as he tried to adjust his hold on the baby, his grip faltered, and he tumbled from the branches, crashing to the forest floor, wrapping himself around Elara.

Sylvan: "No, Elara!"

Taking the brunt of the fall, Sylvan checked to make sure Elara wasn't hurt. Before he could recover, a group of demons descended upon him, stealing Elara from his grasp, and knocking him unconscious.

Elara's cries echoed through the forest, piercing the very soul of those who heard. The demons handed Elara to Malachar, and seizing the opportunity Malachar reached out with his staff, and stole the infant's soul. The air grew heavy with Elara's anguish, her body left empty and lifeless.

Malachar: "Foolish creatures, your time has come!"

Malachar, a sinister smile played on his lips, as he offered a chilling proposition to Borealis, "Release your soul to me, and I will return the child unharmed."

Borealis thundered, "Release her! I will give you what you want!"

Malachar: "You've got yourself a deal."

Borealis took flight, shrinking himself down to the size of a coin, and flew into the jewel on Malachar's staff.

As Elara's soul was released, a radiant light enveloped her form, and she was cast away to the safety of her parents as she began to cry.

Amelia, her eyes filled with tears of desperation and relief, reached out, and opened an ancient tree trunk that acted as a portal. She channeled her energy to send Elara to Eudora.

Amelia: "Elara, be safe, my little dew drop...I love you with all of my heart." Amelia took off her amulet and sent it with Elara before encasing her in the trees.

With Elara secured, Amelia and Erik turned their attention to Malachar. But with Borealis' powers now at his disposal, he had become a formidable force.

Borealis, once radiant and powerful, now found himself trapped within the staff's nightmarish confines. His light began to dim, and the colors of his essence faded, like a fire quenched by a relentless storm.

As the last vestiges of Borealis' essence were sucked into the staff, a transformation swept over Malachar. The stench of rot and decay that had clung to him began to dissipate, carried away by an otherworldly wind.

The forest, once vibrant with life and color, succumbed to an eerie darkness as if a veil of shadow had been drawn over it. The once-cloudless sky became dark and cloudy, like an omen of impending doom.

Malachar's form underwent a startling metamorphosis. His hunched, old, and decaying body began to straighten and rejuvenate. His skin regained its youthful suppleness, and his eyes, once clouded with age, now glowed with vitality. He shed the tattered robes of the old shaman, which disintegrated into ash, revealing a new, darkly ornate attire.

With every passing moment, Malachar grew stronger, a force of darkness and malevolence more powerful than ever before. The stolen power of Borealis coursed through him, and it was as though the very essence of the forest itself had become an extension of his newfound strength.

In the wake of this transformation, the forest groaned, as if in mourning for the life and light that had been stolen from it. The once-lively creatures fell silent, and the vibrant colors turned to shades of gray, like a world caught in the grip of a never-ending twilight.

As the dark storm clouds swirled overhead, Malachar, now a vibrant and imposing figure, looked upon his altered reflection in a crystal-clear pool. A smile of wicked satisfaction curved his lips, as he reveled in the stolen power, fully aware of the devastation he had wrought upon the once beautiful realm. The forest was forever changed, and Malachar had ascended to a new level of dark, formidable power.

Amelia's eyes blazed like emerald fire as her magic surged through her. The very essence of the forest responded to her call. Vines, rocks, branches, insects, and animals became her allies, launching themselves at Malachar from every direction, like an unstoppable force of elemental rage.

Erik, recognized the storm of power his wife had unleashed, took shelter behind the closest tree, his heart pounding with a mix of fear and admiration.

Amelia's voice rang out like thunder, echoing through the forest, "MALACHAR!"

Malachar, standing amid the impending chaos, couldn't help but laugh in the face of the tempest, "You've got a little fire in you for an earth emberlyn." With a deft movement of his staff, Malachar brought everything to an astounding standstill. The tempest of nature's wrath was frozen in time, suspended like an intricate painting, every detail hanging mid-air.

Malachar's eyes blazed with dark power as he swung his staff in Amelia's direction. His voice, resonating with a sinister command, boomed through the stillness, "TAKE HER!"

At his bidding, demons and shadows surged forward, closing in on Amelia and Erik. The forest, once a sanctuary, became a sinister trap, engulfing them in total darkness.

Amidst the inky abyss, a vision of Malachar taunted them, his voice a chilling echo, "You haven't seen anything yet! Banish them to the shadow realm."

The world around them twisted and contorted, like a nightmare come to life. Trees contorted into grotesque shapes, the ground shifted beneath their feet, and the sky became a maelstrom of chaotic colors. The air itself felt oppressive as if it were trying to crush their very souls. In this nightmarish landscape of torment and despair, Amelia and Erik clung to each other, their determination to escape the shadow realm their only flicker of hope in the suffocating darkness.

Amelia: "Erik, hold on! We'll find a way back!"

Erik, pulled his wife tighter to him, "We'll get through this, Amelia, together!"

Sylvan, awakening from his fall, rushed back to the battle just in time to witness the abduction of Amelia and Erik. His heart ached with despair as he watched them vanish, their desperate cries echoing in the fading light. The once-lively forest had fallen into a shroud of darkness and the future uncertain.

Sylvan collapsed to the ground in despair, crying, "No, I couldn't save them... but this isn't over. While I live and breathe, Malachar won't win!"

Looking over the battlefield, at the wanton destruction and lifelessness, Sylvan suddenly jumped to his feet looking around frantically, "Elara!?! Oh no...Elara where are you? I've got to find her..."

As Sylvan began his search for Elara, the vision faded into nothingness, bringing a deafening silence to the trio.

Chapter 6

The Hidden Grove now harbored the weight of Elara's grief. The memory of her parents played before her eyes like a haunting specter, leaving her heart shattered. After the scene unfolded, her knees gave way, and she crumpled to the Grove floor.

Amidst her tears, her mother's amulet slipped from her neck and fell with a soft chime. Sylvan, who had been watching the memory unfold, caught the glint of the amulet and a realization dawned upon him.

Sylvan: "Elara… you're….. Amelia's daughter."

Elara lost in her pain, looked up at Sylvan, her eyes a mixture of sorrow and anger, "My parents… they suffered so much. How could this happen to them?"

Sylvan, his voice a gentle caress, moved closer to Elara and placed a comforting paw on her shoulder, "I'm so sorry, Elara."

Elara, in the throes of her grief, felt a surge of anger bubbling within her. The Grove, sensing her turmoil, responded. The air crackled with energy, and the leaves rustled in sympathy. Elara stood, "It's not fair! They didn't deserve this. None of us do!"

As Elara's emotions intensified, the glow of her powers manifested around her. Her flickering aura around her transformed into a swirling vortex of untamed magic, creating a tempest of energy that whipped the air into a frenzy. The winds spiraled around her, pulling everything in their chaotic dance.

Rascal, clinging to a nearby branch, shouted with increased urgency, "Kid! Kid! Calm down!"

Sylvan shouted over the roar of the wind, "Elara! I know you're upset. You need to control yourself. We will find a way to fix this."

Elara collapsed to her knees once more, tears streaming down her face. "But my parents..." she choked out. As if in response to her overwhelming sorrow, the raging wind gradually subsided, and a soft rain began to descend from the darkened sky, its gentle patter echoing the quiet turmoil within Elara's heart.

Sylvan and Rascal walked over to Elara and engulfed her in a hug.

Just then, the once crystal-clear water of the waterfall began to transform. Its pristine flow turned dark as an inky blackness spread through the water like a stain. A thick, eerie fog crept over the serene lake as the air grew heavy.

It was then, that a chilling vision materialized before them. Malachar emerged from the shadows, his eyes gleaming.

Malachar: "Ah, Elara. What a delightful reunion. Your tears are like music to my ears."

Elara, her eyes burning, faced the vision of Malachar.

Sylvan, shifting to stand in front of Elara, "What do you want, Malachar?"

Malachar: "Ahhhh Sylvan, the Almighty Gatekeeper, I don't know why you're here, the last time I saw you, you were running with your tail between your legs. I have no business with you."

Sylvan: "That's not what happened and you know it. And if you're sooooooo powerful, how come you have to appear in a vision, too afraid to talk face to face?"

Malachar rolled his eyes before shifting his gaze to Elara, "Elara, my sweet, it has been too long."

Elara: "What do you want?"

Malachar: "I want to make a deal with you…… to help you out. A girl shouldn't go her whole life without seeing her parents."

Elara glared at Malachar, "What are you talking about?"

Malachar walked over to Elara wrapping his arm around her shoulder, "I can't imagine how hard it has been for you, what it was like struggling in the bakery with Grammy, working your little hands to the bone, while all the other little boys and girls got to play their little hearts out. Well, you say the word and I'll have your parents back home by sundown."

Rascal scoffed, "Your words are just pretty lies, you old bag of bones. Elara, don't listen to him. He's just blowing smoke."

Sylvan glared at the vision, "You're becoming desperate in your isolation aren't you Malachar?"

Elara: "And what's in it for you?"

Malachar: "Right to business, you know that's the problem with you children, it's all about the destination, but the journey, my dear, is the best part. But now that you mention it, there is one tinsy winsy little thing that I need from you to make it all come true. I need you to leave my forest and never come back." Malachar grinned at Elara.

Elara stiffened as she met the worried looks of Sylvan and Rascal.

Malachar: "Just think, Elara, you could be one big happy family again."

With a flick of his wrist, Malachar showed a vision of Amelia baking with Eudora. Erik dancing in the kitchen with Elara. Laughing and joking around. Amelia throws flour at Erik before a mini food fight commences. The four sit around the fireplace as Erik tells a story.

Malachar whispered in Elara's ear, "Doesn't it look just cozy?"

Elara: "I've never seen grandma so happy."

Sylvan and Rascal share an uneasy look at one another.

The vision dissipated and Malachar looked at Elara, his hand out in front of her, "Do we have a deal?"

Elara raised her hand almost to shake hands with Malachar then removed her hand, paused, and looked at Sylvan and Rascal, "Why does it matter if I leave the forest?"

Sylvan: "He knows you're the only one who can stop him, Elara."

Malachar grinned, "Nonsense, the forest is just a dangerous place for a child, and I'd never forgive myself if you got hurt."

Rascal: "The only danger in this forest is you."

Malachar ignored Rascal's comment, and reached out his hand, "So, we got a deal?"

Elara: "No."

Malachar was shocked, "What do you mean NO? This is what you always wanted right?"

Elara: "Not like this."

Malachar: "This is my final offer."

Elara, though torn by the prospect of freeing her parents, stood firm, glaring at Malachar, "My parents wouldn't want this. They won't give up and neither will I. No deal…"

Sylvan took a breath of relief and smiled with pride.

Malachar snarled, his tone turned sinister, as he leaned closer to her, "Very well, Elara. As you wish, just remember that I tried to save you from this fate."

Rascal: "Fat chance, soul sucker. Be like a tree and leaf."

Elara, fueled by a newfound strength, faced the looming threat with unwavering resolve exclaimed, "I won't let you destroy everything I have left. We'll fight you, no matter what it takes."

Malachar smirked, "Your mother had the same fire in her, and you see where that got her. I'll see you soon."

The vision of Malachar dissipated, leaving the grove in an eerie silence.

Sylvan, moving to wrap Elara in another hug, "Your mother would be proud." turning to Rascal, "We'll rest here for a few days. We'll be safe here. With the Grove sealed no darkness can enter. Borealis saw to that. Tomorrow, Elara, we'll continue your training. Help me set up camp Rascal."

Rascal placed his paw on Elara's shoulder, "You did good kid. I'll go get some firewood and see if I can rustle up some grub."

Elara, eyes glistening with unshed tears, looked at her friends, "Thank you..for.. everything."

The duo smile and nod before setting out to start camp.

A little while later they all sat around a small fire, munching on the berries, nuts, and fish Rascal had found.

Rascal burped, "Ahh that was good."

Sylvan rolled his eyes, "You're just as uncouth as ever."

Rascal: "We both can't be sticks in the mud."

Elara chuckled at the two as they continued to lightly bicker with each other, "We'll continue my training tomorrow, right Sylvan?"

Sylvan: "Yes, Elara we will. For now, I suggest we all get a good night's sleep. It's been a trying day. We could all use it. I'll do a perimeter walk before I tuck in."

Sylvan got up from his place by the fire to walk the perimeter of the Grove.

Elara called after him, "Goodnight Sylvan."

Sylvan nodded in her direction before setting off.

Elara watched Sylvan leave, "Perimeter walk? Rascal, I thought he said we'd be safe tonight?"

Rascal: "Don't worry kid. He just needs to do something. He's restless. Today took a toll on him."

Elara looked over at Rascal confused, "What do you mean?"

Rascal: "He hasn't been the same since he lost all of you."

Rascal noticed Elara's shocked expression, "You really don't know, do you?"

Elara: "What don't I know?"

Rascal sighed deeply as he scratched his chest, "Sylvan blames himself for that day. He lost everything that mattered to him. He lost his mentor, his best friend, and his godchild."

Elara: "I'm Sylvan's godchild?"

Rascal: "Who better to look after the newest Champion of the Forest, than its mighty Gatekeeper?"

Elara: "I had no idea."

Rascal: "There's no way you would have known you were just a baby. He's probably restless now because, for the first time in years, he has hope. You did that. You know we haven't seen many emberlyns in the past years, but all the best ones not only control an element but also convey a message. And I think that's what he sees in you."

Elara: "But what about……."

Rascal held up a paw, "Let's talk more in the morning, let's get some shut-eye kid, we have a long journey ahead of us."

Elara: "Goodnight Rascal."

Rascal: "Goodnight Elara."

After a few hours, Elara woke after hearing a faint noise. She opened her eyes to see Rascal on his back snoring with his legs on a log, with berries and nutshells all over his body.

Elara shifted to stand shaking her head at the raccoon.

Elara: "At least one of us can sleep."

Looking to the spot that Sylvan had claimed, only to see he was not there. Elara set out to look for him.

Elara left the campsite and headed towards the waterfall where the noise came from. There, Elara found Sylvan staring into the sparkling water.

Sylvan sat perched on a stump, fidgeting with pebbles as he occasionally tossed them into the falls. *That accounts for the noise I heard,* thought Elara as she neared Sylvan.

Elara: "Sylvan, are you alright?

Sylvan not turning to look at her, "You know I did everything I could that day. I tried to protect you. To keep you safe and out of their grasp. You know that don't you?"

Elara: "I know Sylvan. I know."

Turning to face her with a tear in his eye, Sylvan expressed, "If I had known, Elara, that you were alive… I wouldn't have stayed away. I would have been there. You were my responsibility. I promised Amelia I'd take care of you. I looked for you. I did. I never thought you made it out of the forest… I am so sorry Elara… It's my fault…"

Elara wrapped Sylvan in a comforting hug, squeezing just a little tighter, "Sylvan, you did everything you could do. I saw what you did. You were so brave. You couldn't have known what would happen. We are going to get them back."

Sylvan smiled, "For the first time in a long time I believe that."

Elara smiled softly, "Let's go back to camp and get some sleep."

As they began their journey back to camp, a soft blue glow appeared to the side.

Elara: "Sylvan, what is that?"

Sylvan turned to look at the light, and gasped, "It's a wisp! They're disembodied spirits who have become one with nature. It's been said that if you should follow, they will lead you to your fate."

Elara pointed, "Look, there's more…"

Sure enough, there was a trail of wisps leading back towards the waterfall.

Elara: "Should we follow the trail?"

Sylvan: "Best not to anger the spirits. Let's see what they want to tell us."

Elara and Sylvan approached the waterfall at the heart of the grove. Its waters cascaded down from a rocky ledge, forming a curtain of liquid crystals that shimmered with an otherworldly radiance. Moonbeams danced upon the surface, revealing a hidden path, and inviting them to ascend.

Hand in hand, Elara and Sylvan stepped onto the glistening stones that led them upward, each step resonating with a mysterious energy. The air hummed with ancient magic as they ascended the waterfall, water parting around them like a liquid staircase. Moonlit droplets hung in the air, creating a luminous veil that surrounded them.

As they reached the summit, a hidden chamber behind the waterfall revealed itself. The space pulsed with an ethereal glow, and the sound of water seemed to transform into an ancient melody. Elara felt a tingling in the air, a presence that extended beyond the physical realm.

In the heart of the chamber, a vision appeared, an ancient tapestry of voices that transcended time. It was the Moirai, the

Fates, the Weavers of Destiny, their forms shifting like shadows with Malachar.

Moirai (in unison):
"In the whispering waters, secrets unfold,
A tale of power, a prophecy foretold.
Malachar, the voodoo shaman dark,
Seeks dominion, to leave his mark.
A bargain struck with destiny's thread,
Ultimate power, the forest bled.
Borealis, the radiant soul,
The key to power, the ultimate goal.
Yet heed our warning, shaman bold,
In Elara's fight, the tale retold.
A choice to make, a destiny true,
In the young one's hands, the forest's cue."

As the prophecy unfolded, Elara and Sylvan stood in silence. The waters seemed to hold the echoes of ancient wisdom, the words resonating in the chamber like a chant.

In the vision, Malachar appeared before the Moirai, a gleam of anticipation in his sunken eyes.

Malachar: "Tell me, Moirai, how do I secure Borealis' soul?"

The Moirai responded:
"Secure the soul of radiant light,
In the battle's heart, darkness fights.
But beware, shaman, heed our call,
If Elara fights, you shall fall."

Malachar, fueled by greed, grinned with satisfaction, walking away paying no attention to their warning.

Elara and Sylvan, still in the chamber, exchanged a knowing look. The prophecy lingered in the air, a tapestry woven with threads of fate, and Elara felt the weight of her destiny pressing upon her.

Elara: "The forest's fate is in my hands, Sylvan. We must face Malachar, and I must fight."

Sylvan nodded, his eyes reflecting the moonlight's glow.

Suddenly, the atmosphere shifted, and shadows coalesced into ethereal forms. The Moirai materialized before Elara and Sylvan, their figures fluid and mysterious, like the wisps of a dream-given life.

Elara felt a chill run down her spine as the words resonated in the air. The Moirai's voices seemed to echo from distant eons, and their eye held the weight of ages.

Moirai (in unison):
  "In this chamber of destiny's lore,
  Two seekers bold, the truth implore.
  Ask of us one question fair,
  In honest words, the answer we share."

Elara, nervously stepping forward, gazed at the Moirai, her eyes filled with a mix of curiosity and trepidation, "How do we save the forest, and free Borealis from the grasp of Malachar?"

The Moirai responded:
"To free the soul, the radiant light,
Malachar's staff must face its plight.
Destroy the vessel, break the chain,
Release the captive, end the bane.
But heed this warning, seekers dear,
Shadows gather, whispers near.
Malachar's minions, sent with spite,
Hunt the seekers in the night."

As the final words lingered in the air, the Moirai dissolved into the moonlit mist, leaving Elara and Sylvan with the weight of newfound knowledge. Elara, her mind brimming with determination, turned to Sylvan, "We must find a way to destroy Malachar's staff. It's the key to freeing Borealis and saving the forest."

Sylvan nodded in agreement, "We will Elara. Let us return to camp. We'll need our rest for what lies ahead."

Chapter 7

Morning struck as Sylvan and Elara began their training amidst the emerald hues of the Hidden Grove. Elara's magic had evolved into a tempest of energy swirling beneath her fingertips. The very ground responded to her will, shaping and bending with newfound mastery.

Sylvan, his eyes gleaming with pride, guided Elara through intricate maneuvers, pushing her limits, "Yes! Yes, Elara! Well done my girl!"

Elara, panting from the exertion, smiled, "I've had a good teacher." Elara unleashed torrents of magic, creating earthen sculptures and manipulating the flora around her.

The air resonated with the raw power she commanded, but even as she marveled at her newfound strength, a hint of uncertainty lingered in her gaze.

Rascal, perched on a nearby branch, chirped in approval, his eyes reflecting the satisfaction of a successful training session, "You're getting the hang of it! We might pull this off!"

Sylvan, his voice resonating like a soothing melody, added his encouragement, "Your magic is stronger than ever. Now, let's take a break. We have to get moving soon. We've lingered here too long."

Elara: "Where do we go next?"

Sylvan: "We will have to venture into the Hollows. It's on the outskirts of the Forest. Beyond the Hollows is the Obsidian Swamp which leads to the Caverns where we can find the entrance of Malachar's Lair."

Rascal shuddered, "That swamp is nasty. It's not the animals I'm worried about, it's the diseases. I had an Aunt go there once she came back rabid."

Sylvan: "Well unlike you Rascal, Elara and I wash ourselves more than once a month so I'm sure that we will be fine."

Rascal lifted his arms and took a whiff, "You may have a point there."

Elara: "Is there no other way to go?"

Sylvan: "I'm afraid not, young one. It is the most direct way to the Caverns, where Malachar calls home."

Elara sighed before taking a drink from her flask, "How long until we reach them?"

Rascal: "A few days as the crows fly."

Elara raised her eyebrow in confusion.

Sylvan answered, "What Rascal means is we will be there in a couple of days."

Rascal: "That's what I said."

The trio emerged from the Hidden Grove, the vibrant canopy giving way to a somber journey.

As they walked further away from the Grove the air grew heavy with the stench of death, decay creeping from the shadows that clung to the trees.

Sylvan: "We must stay alert from here on in. The closer we get to the Caverns, the more likely our enemy will show their hand. Keep up Rascal! I will leave you behind!"

Rascal in a mocking tone struggled to keep up, "I will leave you behind. It's not my fault you walk like a Djinn. Honestly, you'd think a pack of angry hell hounds were on your tail the way you move!"

Sylvan: "And it's not MY fault that you decided to have a fourth helping at breakfast!"

Elara laughed breathlessly, "Come on you two! Let's go!"

The days flew by as the trio traveled through the woods. As Sylvan and Rascal bickered, Elara found herself lost in thought.

She thought about what the Moirai had said, about the vision she had seen of her parents, about how much she missed her grandmother and hoped that she was ok.

The breeze blew through her hair and whispered: *Be safe, stay warm, be wary.*

Before Elara could contemplate the words that came from the breeze, Sylvan had caught up to her.

Sylvan: "We've arrived. Behold the Hollows."

As the trio approached the outskirts the air grew thick with an oppressive stillness, and an eerie silence enveloped the desolate landscape. The Hollows stretched out before them like a vast expanse of forgotten dreams and forsaken hopes.

The sky above seemed perpetually cloaked in a shroud of charcoal-gray clouds, blocking any trace of sunlight from penetrating the despondent atmosphere. The very air felt heavy, laden with the weight of a thousand lost souls.

The once vibrant colors of the surrounding flora were now muted as if a spectral hand had drained the life force from every living thing.

The trees, skeletal remnants of their former selves. Their leaves long turned to a sickly shade of ashen brown, rustled in the melancholic breeze that whispered through the barren branches. It was a symphony of desolation, the mournful soundtrack of a land abandoned by the warmth of vitality.

The ground beneath their feet was cracked and dry, the soil devoid of any sign of life. The Hollows seemed to hunger for the essence of existence, an insatiable void that had swallowed all traces of life and vitality.

The very Earth itself seemed to groan under the weight of despair as if mourning the loss of something beautiful that could never be restored.

A dim, sickly light emanated from the distance, casting long, distorted shadows that danced along the edges of the forlorn landscape. It was a light that offered no comfort, only serving to accentuate the desolation that permeated every inch of the Hollows.

An eerie feeling of being watched sent shivers down their spines.

Rascal: "Anyone else got the feeling we're being watched? No? Just me?"

Sylvan: "Rascal you could wake the dead with the racket you're making."

Rascal: "What? You can't tell me you don't feel eyes on you!"

Rascal shivered, his fur standing on edge, "Look! The fur never lies. We're being watched."

Elara's eyes scope the landscape before whispering, "Not watched…hunted."

Suddenly, they were surrounded by howls, and shadows materialized into the form of sinister creatures – the Shadow Wolves, demons bound to Malachar's will.

A deep voice boomed over the snarls and soft growls, "Clever little thing, aren't you?"

Sylvan: "Fenrir…"

The leader of the Shadow Wolves emerged, he was a massive creature, his eyes gleamed crimson red.

Fenrir: "Well well well boys. Look what we've found. A couple of trespassers."

The pack of wolves snickered and cackled in response.

Sylvan stood stiff, "This doesn't have to be a fight Fenrir."

Fenrir prowled closer, "Oh, dear, sweet, innocent Sylvan, but it does."

Fenrir grinned, baring his fangs, "Look fellas it looks like our little Sylvan made some friends……too bad for the lot of you. Things don't work out too well when you get close to this one."

Fenrir looked at Elara, "You're out of your league here, why don't you go back home before you get hurt."

Elara scoffed, "Home? Why would I go home when I can stay here and enjoy your charming company?"

Fenrir snickered, turning his attention to Rascal, "Oooooh how nice, you guys brought me a snack."

Rascal scoffed, "Snack? Did a field mouse whisper that into your oversize ears? I'm not some lowly nibble; I'm the feast of legends. If you're searching for a main course look no further. You're staring right at it, though I doubt those dull senses of yours could discern fine dining from a rock."

Fenrir lunged at Rascal, fangs bared and claws outstretched; when suddenly a boulder smashed into his side sending him into the trees.

Elara's eyes widened with excitement, "Oops, sorry about that."

Sylvan chuckled, eyes alight with pride, "Good. Now let's take care of the rest!"

Fenrir picking himself up from where he was thrown snarled, "GET THEM!"

The rest of the wolves descended upon the group. Their numbers grew by the second. The battle unfolded in a frenzied swarm of chaos. The Shadow Wolves, their fur as dark as midnight, circled the trio with predatory intent.

Rascal looked to Sylvan, "May the best raccoon win."

Sylvan shook his head before delving into the fray.

Sylvan: "Come at me you mangy mutts!"

Sylvan landed a right hook to the closest wolf, knocking out a fang. He then hopped onto the next wolf's back as two more barreled towards them. Just as they were about to grab him from the back of their comrade, Sylvan leaped off causing the three wolves to collide.

Sylvan: "Come on, it's like you're not even trying. Elara do try and keep up."

Rascal: "Alright Sylvan! Show 'em! YIKES!" Rascal took off running up a tree with three wolves nipping at his tail.

Rascal: "Easy boys! You don't want me! I'm gamey!"

"I've got you Rascal," Elara shouted as vines wrap around the legs of the wolves that were reaching for Rascal, whipping them back towards the ground.

Rascal: "Whew, thanks kid. Look out behind you."

Turning to face her new opponents, Elara waved her arms in a wide arc, creating a wave of rocks that knocked the approaching wolves off their feet with a yelp.

Sylvan: "Well done! Keep going!"

Fenrir: "You're mine Gatekeeper! Let's finish this!"

Seizing the moment, Fenrir lunged, crashing into Sylvan and sending them both sprawling to the ground.

Elara: "Sylvan! NO!" Elara's arm stretched as if reaching to pull Sylvan from the ground herself, creating barriers and striking the ground to destabilize her adversaries.

With Fenrir distracted, Sylvan maneuvered skillfully, slipping his hands and feet beneath him. In a deft move, he tosses Fenrir overhead into the midst of the pack.

The wolves, growing into a massive swarm, were swift and cunning, their dark forms weaving through the onslaught.

Elara: "Sylvan, we can't keep this up! They're too fast!"

Sylvan, deflecting attacks, struggled to maintain their defense, "We need to regroup! Head for the clearing!"

Fenrir: "Leaving so soon? The fun is just getting started." The pack surged towards the trio blocking all paths to safety.

Taking advantage of the pack's distraction, Fenrir swiftly moved toward Elara, delivering a powerful headbutt that brought her to the ground. Elara grunted in pain as she hit the ground.

Sylvan raced toward Fenrir and Elara. He grabbed Fenrir's tail and threw him into his pack. As the wolf is wrenched away, Elara felt the sting of Fenrir's claws deep in her back.

Sylvan helped her to her feet. As she stood Elara felt the dampness of blood from her wounds. Wincing, Elara said, "We can't keep this up…"

Sylvan: "We have to try….."

Rascal: "Guys……I don't mean to ruin this seemingly tender moment, but will one of you get rid of these wolves so I can get down from this tree!"

Sylvan: "Keep your fur on we're coming," Sylvan turned to look at Elara, "Shall we?"

Elara, in her determined stance, channeled the very elements to respond to her will. Vines surged forth from the Earth, entwining with the Shadow Wolves, ensnaring them in a tangle of nature's grasp. The ground beneath them trembled as if mirroring the tumult within Elara's heart.

Sylvan gracefully maneuvered through the chaos. His movements, a ballet of evasion and counterattack, each step a testament to his agility and skill. With a swift swipe of his tail, he deflected an oncoming wolf, while his keen eyes scanned the battlefield for strategic opportunities.

Rascal, not to be outdone, darted down the tree and weaved between wolves, a nimble trickster amid the fray. His sharp claws and teeth found their mark, adding a layer of chaos to the already frenzied scene.

Each clash of fang and claw, every burst of magic, resonated through the ancient trees as if the very spirits of the forest were watching in awe.

As Elara watched her friends endure the relentless assault, a surge of raw emotion welled up within her as she lost control.

Elara: "Enough!" The ground beneath her trembled as Elara erupted, creating a shock wave that reverberated through the clearing. Stones rose from the Earth, forming a protective barrier around her, while vines lashed out, ensnaring the Shadow Wolves. The very Earth seemed to rebel against their intrusion.

Elara: "Stay back!"

The wolves yelped and recoiled, subdued by the force of nature itself. Fenrir growled defiantly, "Impressive, little emberlyn. But you cannot escape the grasp of the shadows."

Elara, her eyes blazing with determination, stepped forward, "Our fight is not with you, Fenrir. Leave now, or face the consequences."

Fenrir: "Oh, you wound me. Hahaha! Little Emberlyn, should you continue on this journey, it won't be laughter that echoes in the end. Consequences will befall you, and the tale you're weaving might not have the happy ending you desire."

Fenrir reared back letting out a deafening howl before vanishing like smoke.

The wolves around them let loose their howls before sinking into the shadows.

The silence that followed echoed with the aftereffects of the battle.

Elara: "Where did they go?"

Rascal: "Probably crawling back to their master, tails tucked between their legs like the pups they are."

Sylvan: "I wouldn't be so sure Rascal. We haven't seen the last of Fenrir or his pack. However, we've shown that we won't be taken down so easily. It's getting late. We need to make camp and clean our wounds. Especially you, Elara, those claw marks need to be cleaned."

Rascal: "I know just the thing for those. Some mud mixed with a little bit of pine sap should help heal those right up."

As the group started making camp, high up in the treetops, Nightshade was perched.

Nightshade: "An Emberlyn?? I thought they were all gone… This is not good. Not good at all. Master isn't going to like this one bit."

Detaching from his perch, Nightshade took flight, still muttering to himself, "Master will want to know Fenrir didn't finish them off. Maybe he'll throw him into the pit! Oh, that would be love….oooooohhhh gooseberries!"

Flying to the gooseberry bush Nightshade gorged himself on the sweet berries. As he was pleasantly munching away, a dark whisper was heard, "Enjoying yourself?"

Nightshade cried out in shock, "Master! Oh Master, I was just flying to give you a report!"

Malachar whacked Nightshade from the bush, "Really, because from where I stand it looked like you were just filling your gullet."

Nightshade flew to Malachar's feet holding onto his shoe for dear life, "Master, oh master I am sorry, I truly was. I got distracted. You know I love gooseberries..the red ones are my favorite, you know Master. The green ones are just too sour and make your lips pucker. But the red ones are so sweet and delectable…"

Malachar: "Get on with it, what have you learned?"

Nightshade: "Oh yes Master. The human isn't a human at all. She's an Emberlyn. The Gatekeeper is training her, Master. He and that raccoon. Oh Master!"

Nightshade chuckled nervously, "Master, are you okay?"

Malachar rolled his eyes in irritation, "An emberlyn huh?" SMACK! "You fool! I knew this! Your job is to provide me with something USEFUL! Not tell me what I already know! Don't bother returning until you've made yourself of some use."

Malachar disappeared into a sea of smoke leaving Nightshade in the woods.

Nightshade: "Master are you there?" Nightshade looked

around and flew into the smoke, "I better head back to the cave to make sure that the Master is ok, he seemed so angry, but a few more gooseberries won't hurt." Nightshade flew back to the gooseberry bush and continued feeding.

Chapter 8

Deep inside his lair, the air thick with the scent of magical concoctions, Malachar worked diligently over his cauldron. The glow of the potions reflected in his cold, calculating eyes. Nightshade flew anxiously to Malachar.

Nightshade: "Master, I never finished my report. They did it! Elara and her friends, they defeated the wolves!"

Malachar's eyes glowed brighter as he continued his work, seemingly undisturbed by the news.

Malachar: "They were just meant to test the girl, not to defeat them, you twittering idiot."

Nightshade: "But Master, what do we do now?"

Malachar's eyes gleamed with a sinister resolve, "We change the rules of the game, Nightshade. We exploit their bonds and dismantle them from within."

Nightshade: "But Master, this is bad! If they can defeat Fenrir, they might pose a real threat to your plans!"

Malachar smirked with a sinister gleam in his eyes, "Oh, my dear Nightshade, don't underestimate the power of desperation. Their victory is but a fleeting illusion."

As Nightshade fidgeted, Malachar pulled out a vial and poured the potion that he was concocting inside.

Malachar: "Take this. A drop of this in the Gatekeeper's mouth while he slumbers. It will be a pleasant surprise for our dear Elara."

Nightshade hesitated, eyeing the vial nervously, "But, Master?"

Malachar: "You will do as you're told, or suffer far worse than the pit you fear so much."

Nightshade: "What does it do?"

Malachar's lips curled into a malicious smile, "It suppresses the essence of magic. A fitting punishment for meddling in my affairs."

Nightshade, though uneasy, took the vial. With the potion in tow, he darted into the night, leaving the cavern behind.

In the serene camp, nestled beneath the trees, Elara, Rascal, and Sylvan slept soundly, exhausted from the earlier battle. The night air was crisp, carrying a gentle breeze that whispered through the leaves. Unbeknownst to them, Nightshade approached like a shadowy wraith.

Nightshade whimpering frantic and out of breath, "Just get the potion into the Gatekeeper, Nightshade. That's it. That's all you have to do." Flapping his wings wearily as he approached the camp, "Just a bit more, Nightshade. You've got this," he muttered, wiping the sweat from his brow with a trembling wing. Dipping to the side, he fumbled, and the vial slipped from his clammy claws, lost amidst the drops of sweat.

Nightshade: "Oh Nightshade now, you've done it!"

Diving after the vial, Nightshade frantically tried to grab the vial with his claws and pulled out the stopper. His eyes widened in panic and alarm, "I'm dead. SO very very dead."

Panting, he swoops down and managed to grab a hold of the vial. He landed on a branch. Looking at the vial clutched tightly in his claws, "Oh no..it's almost gone. Master's hard work ruined. I hope a drop does the trick..."

Hovering over Sylvan, who laid in a restful slumber, Nightshade carefully released the drop of the potion into his mouth and flew off into the night. As the liquid touched Sylvan's tongue, a dark aura surrounded him, unseen by the unsuspecting trio.

The tranquility of the night shattered as Sylvan's peaceful slumber turned into anguished screams. Elara and Rascal jolted awake, panic etched on their faces.

Elara: "Sylvan! What's happening?"

Rascal, wide-eyed, frantically looked around saw the wavering speck of Nightshade's retreating form. Nightshade's chilling laughter echoed in the air as he vanished into the shadows.

As they watched in horror, the vibrant colors that defined Sylvan began to fade. His once luminous aura dimmed, and he shrank down to the size of a regular squirrel. The transformation was complete, leaving behind a small, ordinary creature where the great Gatekeeper once laid.

Elara, bewildered, reached out to the now diminutive Sylvan. Her fingers trembled as they made contact feeling his vulnerability, "No, this can't be happening! Rascal, what's going on?"

Sylvan's now tiny paws clutching Elara's fingers as he chattered in reply. His eyes, once filled with wisdom, now mirrored confusion and fear. Sylvan's head snapped to the side as an acorn caught his eye. Without a moment's hesitation, he darted towards it, leaving his friends in his wake.

Elara cried out after him, "Sylvan where are you going?! Come back here!"

Rascal, his eyes filled with sorrow, stepped forward, "Let him go, Elara."

Elara: "What?! Rascal are you crazy? He could get hurt! What do you mean "Let him go?!"

Rascal glared at her, "I don't know what they did to him, but I saw a creature flying away, this has Malachar written all over it."

Elara stared at the raccoon in shock, "Rascal, we can fix this… there has to be a way to fix Sylvan….right?"

Rascal huffed gesturing to where Sylvan was frolicking in the leaves, "If there was a way only Sylvan would know and he's not exactly going to be much help is he kid?"

Elara gritted her teeth, "Then WE will just have to figure it out then, won't we."

Rascal sarcastically, "Sure kid. It's hopeless anyway you look at it."

Hours passed as the duo watched as Sylvan raced through the treetops collecting acorns and burying them in the ground.

Elara glanced at Rascal, before cautiously asking, "Rascal, are you alright?"

Rascal, who had been staring into the fire lost in thought jolted, "Huh? What? Oh, yeah. I'm ok kid."

Elara gave Rascal a disbelieving look, "You have two options, you can either sit there like a bump on a log being miserable or you can talk to me and we can figure out a way to get our friend back."

Rascal sighed, "Did I ever tell you how Sylvan and I met?"

Elara, shocked at the vulnerability in his tone, shook her head no.

Rascal kept his gaze on the fire, as he began his tale, "We were brothers. Sylvan's father found me as a baby after my mother died. Sylvan and I were as close as could be."

He continued, recounting the sacrifice of Sylvan's father in the first battle against Malachar, "Sorren, Sylvan's father, was the Gatekeeper when your mother took over as Champion. He showed her how to control her magic, just like Sylvan has with you. When he wasn't training her, he was home with Sylvan and I. Sorren would tell us countless stories of his battles. We would pretend to battle each other with our stick swords and leaf shields under his watchful eye. Serena, Sylvan's mother, would show us the secrets of the forest. She was so warm and caring. Her fur shined like the sun. She made sure to tell us which plants could cure ailments and clean wounds. She was always patching Sorren up."

Elara: "What happened to them?"

Rascal sighed, "Our father gave his life for Borealis"

Elara softly whispered, "How?"

Rascal: "Malachar's corrupting influence on the forest was driven by ambition that nearly led to the forest's downfall. However, his conquest was thwarted when Borealis, Amelia, and Sorren confronted him. As they battled against Malachar, Sorren, recognizing the gravity of the threat, shielded Borealis from a powerful magical onslaught, giving his own life to preserve the balance. This unexpected sacrifice left Borealis and Amelia in shock, altering the course of the battle and ensuring the survival of the forest."

Rascal took a deep breath, looking sadly to where Sylvan was now curled up in the leaves near the fire, "Sylvan became the next Gatekeeper, which meant leaving Mother and I behind. When he returned, our mother was gone, and we had a falling out. We haven't been close since….until you."

Elara, understanding the weight of the shared history, placed a comforting hand on Rascal's shoulder, "We'll get him back, Rascal. We'll find a way to reverse whatever Malachar did."

Rascal looked at Elara, with hope shining briefly in his eyes, "We should head back to the Grove. It'll be safer to try to figure out a way to get him back there than out here in the open. Maybe we'll even find a vision or something to help us figure it out." Rascal looked at Elara's face and saw the exhaustion in her eyes, "Come on kid, it's time for some shut-eye. We'll leave at first light."

Elara nodding in agreement moved over to where Sylvan laid. Curling herself around his tiny body she whispered, "Don't worry Sylvan. We'll fix this."

As dawn broke through the withering trees, Rascal and Elara prepared to go back to the Grove.

Rascal: "Do we have everything?"

Elara looked around her, "I think so…wait…where's Sylvan?"

Rascal's eyes darted around frantically, "What do you mean where's Sylvan? I thought he was with you?!" The sound of rustling leaves erupted between the duo as they both looked down to see Sylvan's head pop out of the pile with an acorn in his mouth.

Rascal sighed in relief, "He's gonna be the death of me. I swear."

Elara bent to pick up the little squirrel before placing him and the acorn in her satchel, "There now, you stay in there Sylvan. You'll be safer and I'll be able to keep an eye on you."

Sylvan chittered in reply before munching on his prize.

A few days passed and the air tingled with uncertainty as they approached the Grove's concealed entrance.

Rascal, scratched his head, "Alright, back to basics. How do we get in now?"

Elara, eyes welled up with tears, "I completely forgot about the entrance. We can't. Oh my God Rascal, we can't get in. What are we going to do?"

Rascal looked uneasy, "Hey, hey, hey. We'll figure it out, Elara. It'll be ok. There has to be a fail-safe or something."

Rascal looked around the entrance to the Grove again, running his fingers over the walls, "Ok Rascal old boy. If Sylvan can open this, you definitely can. Come on. What did he do?"

Rascal placed his arms at his side. Closing his eyes, he took a deep breath, opened his eyes, raised his hands to his heart, and pushed his hands away.

Rascal grumbled, "Oh come on already. That's exactly what he did. Open up."

After trying again with no luck, Rascal began to tear up. Rascal fell to his knees, "We need to get in. We HAVE to get in you stupid Grove! Your Gatekeeper needs your help and you're not going to help?!" Glaring up at the Grove's entrance, Rascal's chest heaved as he tried to control his anger.

Feeling little paws against his leg, Rascal looked down to see Sylvan looking up at him. Sylvan's eyes alight with the wisdom of ages in their hazel depths.

Rascal snorted, "Go ahead, gloat. I can't do anything. Say it, I told you so."

Sylvan shook his head as he climbed up to Rascal's chest, placing his tiny paw over Rascal's heart.

Rascal, wiped his nose with an arm, "What are you doing?"

Sylvan pushed against Rascal's chest before turning to face the entrance. Jumping off, Sylvan sat in front of Rascal, placing his paws over his heart, and pushed outward.

Rascal: "You want me to try again? It won't work. I tried that already. Twice."

Sylvan chattered angrily, kicking at Rascal before gesturing again.

Rascal: "Fine. Fine. Fine! Third time's the charm, right?"

Dusting himself off, Rascal rose to his feet and followed the movements of the tiny Sylvan.

Whispering to himself, "Please let this work, please, please, please."For a moment nothing happened. Rascal sighed in defeat, "See Sylvan? I told you…"

Before he finished his sentence, the wind blew and the waterfall cascaded over the entrance of the Grove as the Groves flora bloomed around the entrance. The mystical barrier to the Hidden Grove dissipated, revealing the vibrant sanctuary within.

Sylvan jumped and ran around the undergrowth chattering and chirping excitedly as Elara joined Rascal. She wiped her eyes and smiles.

Elara: "You did it Rascal. You figured out how to open the Grove…"

Rascal, in awe, looked at his paws, "I did…I really did."

Elara, picking up Sylvan, followed Rascal through the entrance of the Grove before the sanctuary sealed behind them.

Elara looked down at Sylvan, "Don't worry Sylvan, we'll figure out how to fix you."

Rascal: "We need to find some clues or something."

Elara looked towards the falls that once led her to the Moirai.

Elara smiled wide, "I have an idea. Come on, Rascal!"

Grabbing hold of the raccoon, Elara began to race towards the falls.

Rascal: "Yipe! Warn a fella before you grab! Where are we going? I can walk, you know?"

Reaching the falls in no time, Elara looked around for the secret entrance as Rascal, with his paws on his knees, tried to catch his breath, "That's it. Next… time…I'll drag you…see how you feel."

Elara: "Shush Rascal and help me. Sylvan and I found a secret entrance the last time we were here. So there has to be a switch or something…"

Rascal mumbled, "You'd think that but you'd be surprised how often there's not."

They looked until night had fallen in the Grove. Elara and

Rascal decided to take a break to set up camp and find food.

As they rested around the fire, Rascal suddenly sat rigid.

Rascal: "Elara..what is that?"

Elara turned to look behind her. Seeing nothing there, she faces Rascal again, "Rascal, there's nothing there."

Rascal: "No, there's something there kid. I'm not fooling around."

Elara: "Ok, what does it look like?"

Rascal: "Like a little blue fireball…"

Elara shot to her feet, jostling a sleeping Sylvan from his perch on her shoulder, "You see the wisp?! Rascal, we have to follow it!"

Rascal: "Kid! Where are you going? They're going this way!" Rascal shouted after Elara as she raced to the far side of the falls where she had found the entrance before.

Rascal: "They're going behind the falls. Follow me."

Navigating the hidden path behind the thundering falls, Rascal and Elara stepped into a vast cavern bathed in the warm, ancient glow of torchlight. The flames danced with a brilliant glow, casting intricate shadows upon the cavern walls.

Amidst the flickering torches, a mysterious portal took shape, its silver essence veiled in shadows. The air seems to shimmer as wisps aligned themselves near the portal.

The cavern pulsed with an atmosphere of ancient secrets, as if the very walls held the echoes of bygone ages, as the torchlight revealed a passage into realms untouched by time.

Elara: "Rascal, what do you see?"

Rascal: "I think they want us to go through that thing." pointing to the portal.

Elara, moving beside Rascal, took his paw in her hand, "I'm with you Rascal."

Rascal, squeezed tight, "Not to be the voice of reason or anything but let's recap. You want us to follow these little blue fireballs into a mysterious portal shrouded in shadows to go to who knows where that could potentially kill us…"

Elara smiled smugly, "Do you trust me?" With Sylvan tucked securely into her arm, Elara jumped into the portal pulling Rascal along behind her.

As they stepped out of the portal, Rascal sputtered, "What kind of person does that? Asks a question then doesn't wait for a response?! The answer, by the way, is NO. No no no I don't because you do stuff like this! You know raccoons aren't like cats, we just have the one life! What's wrong with you scaring me like that!"

Elara, chuckling, turned her head to see that the Moirai awaited them. The three ancient sisters, draped in robes woven from the threads of fate, observed the trio with a penetrating eye. Elara, with a respectful nod, "We seek your wisdom, mighty Moirai, to restore what was stolen from our friend."

Moirai (in unison)
"A warning spoke, a pledge of peace.
One question asked, a limit reached,
The threads of fate, in silence, breached.
Heed our words, where life strings sway,
Challenge not our ancient way.
For should you persist, in queries vast,
The shears of fate may cut at last."

Rascal looked at Elara, "In layman's terms please?"

Elara: "They're saying that we already asked our question and that if we keep bothering them there will be consequences."

Rascal, stepping forward, "Whoa whoa whoa, hold on just one second ladies. I never asked my question, now did I?"

Moirai (with a hint of irritation):
"A twist in fate, a turn of the game.
One question more, but choose with care,
or answers may bring a weight to bear."

Rascal rubbed his paws together, "Great! Now, about Sylvan's magic, can you tell us how to bring it back?"

The Moirai glanced at Sylvan, their expressions unreadable.
"In this grove, where echoes unfold,
A tale of Sylvan, his magic foretold.
Malachar, with his shadows dark,
Strives for power, to leave his mark.
Beneath moon's glow, a secret lies,
In waters deep, some magic lies.
Sylvan's essence, once bound by strife,
In ancient waters, comes back to life.
Yet heed this warning, in shadows' hold,
To regain his magic, a story retold.
In Sylvan's hands, destiny weaves,
Defeat the shadow, his magic retrieves."

The Moirai cackled before vanishing.

Rascal threw his hands in the air, "Well that's so helpful. Thanks ladies." Rascal looked at Elara, "Did you get any of that?"

Elara: "In waters deep, some magic lies……. Do you think that means that the water in the Grove could help Sylvan?

Rascal: "It can't hurt to try."

Elara, Sylvan, and Rascal made their way down from behind the falls and set up camp near the lake. Elara walked over to the lake to get a drink and looked at her reflection. *I wonder if Grandma would even recognize me anymore, so much has changed,* she thought.

Elara, adorned in her weathered cloak, beared the marks of

her journey etched upon her. Scars across her skin, testaments to battles fought and trials endured. Her eyes, once filled with youthful curiosity, now reflect the wisdom gained through hardship. Cuts and bruises, badges of her resilience, paint a vivid story of her transformation throughout her journey.

The radiant energy of her magic was accompanied by an air of seasoned maturity, a stark contrast to the wide-eyed innocence that marked the beginning of her quest. Each step forward has sculpted her into a formidable force, a beacon of strength against the encroaching shadows.

Elara sat by the water for a while, just thinking, then looked over at Sylvan, getting a drink of water from the lake, and his reflection, "Sylvan look in the water it's you, I mean, of course it's you. It's your reflection but, it's YOU! IN DEEP WATER MAGIC LIES!" Elara ran over to Sylvan, grabbed him eliciting a startled squeak from the tiny creature, and threw him in the middle of the lake.

Rascal: "WHAT ARE YOU INSANE!?!?!?!?!"

Elara: "In deep waters, some magic lies. This is what the fates were telling us. I saw his true self in the waters."

Rascal faced Elara in disbelief, "This is too risky. I'm going in after him."

Elara looked behind Rascal seeing Sylvan come out of the water, "Rascal..."

Rascal: "No he is my brother. This was the most impulsive thing I've ever seen in my life. If you are going to be the Champion you need to think before you act….."

Sylvan walked up behind Rascal, patting him on the shoulder, "You've gotten soft in your old age, old boy."

Rascal turned his head slightly, "Not now Sylvan, this is serious."

Rascal paused, turned around, and leaped in Sylvan's arms, "You're back!"

Elara: "You're brown….?"

Rascal pulled back to look at Sylvan, "He's not…brown…Sylvan, you're not green."

Sylvan looked down at his fur and sighed, "Don't you remember, the Moirai said to restore my magic, we have to defeat Malachar."

Elara walked over to Sylvan and hugged him with a tear in her eye, "It's so good to hear your voice again."

Sylvan: "It feels good to be heard again."

Elara: "Well now that you're back, and the three of us are somewhat back to normal, let's get some rest, we'll be safe here for the night."

Rascal: "I'll go find some grub."

The trio sat around the campfire enjoying each other's company, sharing stories, and laughing while eating dinner.

Elara: "Good night Rascal. Good Night Sylvan."

Rascal: "Goodnight."

Sylvan: "Goodnight."

Elara nodded off and Sylvan turned to Rascal and smiled.

Rascal: "What are you looking at?"

Sylvan: "I just wanted to say I told you so."

Rascal: "About what?"

Sylvan: "I knew you could get us in the Grove. You are capable of so much more than you realize, I just wish you could see that."

Rascal: "If I knew you were going to come back all wishy-washy I wouldn't have brought you back."

Sylvan smiled and turned around, "Goodnight."

Rascal closed his eyes with a giant smile on his face, "Goodnight Sylvan."

Chapter 9

As the first light of dawn painted the sky in hues of pink and gold, Elara, Rascal, and Sylvan gathered their belongings and bid farewell to the Hidden Grove. The rejuvenated Sylvan, now restored to his former size, exuded an air of confidence that matched the lush greenery of the Grove. As they walked along the winding pathways toward the Hollows, the trio began to devise a plan.

Elara: "Where to now?"

Sylvan: "We continue where we left off. Once we get past the Hollows, we'll be in the Obsidian Swamp."

Elara asked, "Are we sure that's such a good idea? You don't have your powers, what if something happens?"

Sylvan: "I appreciate your concern, I'll just have to be more careful, and you have saved our tails a time or two before even with my magic."

Rascal: "Yeah kid, keep an eye out for the old man."

Elara smiled, "I won't let anything happen to the two of you."

The trio ventured through the familiar Hollows, the towering trees standing sentinel as they weaved through the forest paths. Sylvan led the way with a newfound sense of purpose.

As they progressed, the air thickened, and the terrain gradually shifted beneath their feet. The once comforting embrace of the forest transformed into a foreboding landscape, the Obsidian Swamp.

The ground beneath them became soft and squelchy, and the air carried the pungent scent of decay. Wisps of mist slithered among gnarled trees, creating an otherworldly atmosphere.

Sylvan: "Be cautious, the Swamp is not a place to let down your guard."

Elara wrinkled her nose, casting a wary glance at the murky waters that stretched before them, "This place gives me the creeps. Why would anyone choose to live here?"

Rascal eyed the surroundings, "It's the perfect setting for Malachar. This place is as unpleasant as he is. Be careful where you step."

Sylvan, his eyes narrowed, "There's bound to be more of Malachar's minions lurking around."

As they ventured deeper, the ominous stillness of the swamp was shattered by eerie sounds. Strange whispers echoed through the mist. Suddenly, from the shadows emerged a skulk of foxes, their eyes glowing with an unnatural light.

Elara stepped in front of Sylvan and Rascal, "Stay back."

The foxes circled the trio with ghostly ferocity.

The foxes began to charge, as Elara launched a boulder taking out the masses.

One fox manages to dodge the boulder and made his way to the trio when Rascal grabbed a large branch and swings at the fox, sending the fox flying back.

Rascal: "Yeah, take that, there's more where that came from! Who's the prey now?"

Three more foxes charged forward, with a shocked expression, Rascal dropped the branch and ran and hid behind Elara's leg.

Sylvan smirked at Rascal, "I thought there was more where that came from?"

Rascal: "I never said from me."

Elara threw her hands out in front of her, the reeds lashed out, entangling themselves in the legs of the foxes.

Sylvan: "Well done, Elara. Keep it up." Sylvan picked up a branch, looked at Rascal and advanced on the foxes, "May the best squirrel win."

With a battle cry, Sylvan launched himself at the foxes bashing and swatting at them. As Sylvan pushed the foxes back, Rascal grumbled as he picks up another branch.

Rascal: "Stupid squirrel's gonna get himself killed."

Swinging the branch above his head, Rascal cried out, "Come get me you dirty mouse-munchers."

Malachar watched the battle from the comfort of his cauldron, "NO NO NO!" He kicked over the pile of books next to his cauldron.

Nightshade flew over, "Master oh Master don't worry I will pick them up." Nightshade looked into the cauldron, "Oh look Master the Gatekeeper's back…and he's brown."

Malachar grabbed Nightshade squeezing, "Did you not give him all of the potion?"

Nightshade, struggling to breathe, "No… Master I did… I swear. He was changing when I flew away."

Malachar, stroked Nightshade's head in thought, "If she found a way to bring him back, she is more powerful than I realized. We have to end this here."

Dropping Nightshade, Malachar went to the shelf containing the ingredients for his potions.

Malachar: "Where is it? I know that it's here…Aha! Here, let's turn the tables shall we?"

Going back to the cauldron, Malachar poured the vial into the cauldron watching the swirl of the potion mix with the image while reciting his spell,

"Soul-bound spirits, from the abyss rise,
Infuse my minions with shadows' prize.
Grant them strength, twisted and defiled,
In shadows' clutch, their power compile"

Malachar smirked, "Let's see how she handles this."

Suddenly the foxes break from their bondage, growing in size and veracity. They break through the protective barriers that Elara crafted, ripping through the vines, and the reeds.

Rascal: "Elara, I think we have a problem."

Elara: "I think you're right Rascal... Sylvan, what do we do?"

As Elara turned her head to talk to Sylvan, a hoard of foxes bulldozed past Elara grabbing Sylvan by the tail, and jumped into the swamp dragging him to the bottom.

Elara: "SYLVAN NO!!!"

Elara dashed toward the edge of the water, and with a swift, commanding motion, she commanded the swamp to heed her call. Vines, reeds, and underwater flora responded to her command, erupting from the murky depths like a swarm, but the cunning spirits, defied her control, shattering free from the entwining embrace.

Rascal: "ELAR………….."

Elara turned around to see that Rascal has been taken. Before she could react, a third group of foxes stampeded over her.

Malachar, watching from his cauldron, smiled his crooked smile, "That's better!"

As she continues to struggle under the onslaught of foxes, Elara felt herself begin to panic. Tears streamed down her face as their claws dug into her.

Suddenly her mind went blank, and her aura went from a gentle calming glow to a thunderous inferno as the foxes on top of her went flying.

Elara regained her footing, and planted her feet into the soggy ground, anchoring herself to the swamp. Her hands swept through the air. Thick roots erupted, coiling around the creature's form in the water and pulled them back to the surface. The vines tightened, momentarily suspending the foxes in mid-air. The spectral howls echoed as the other foxes hesitated, wary of the sudden display of power.

Undeterred, Elara continued her dance with the Earth. She traced arcane symbols in the air, and from the swampy soil emerged sharp spikes of obsidian. With a forceful command, the spikes shot upward, stabbing the foxes that took Rascal and dragging them back to the swamp. The foxes, now encircled by a jagged fortress, struggled.

With a determined gaze, Elara connected with the roots beneath the swamp's surface. The ground quivered as colossal tendrils emerged, weaving a mesmerizing pattern in the air. The tendrils lashed out bringing Sylvan and Rascal back to Elara and then intertwining with the vines that ensnared the foxes.

"Kid, remind me never to get on your bad side," Rascal quipped.

Elara's focus intensified as she felt the spirits within the foxes resisting her control. She closed her eyes, delving deeper into the swamp's energy.

The tendrils responded to her unspoken plea, pulsating with a gentle luminescence. Slowly, the foxes' struggles ceased as the glow enveloped them.

In a final, fluid motion, Elara released her grip on the Earth. The vines and spikes receded, returning to the swamp's embrace. The foxes, now-freed from their spectral possession, blinked with confusion.

Rascal watched the now freed foxes begin to frolic and play in the reeds and tall grass, their playful yips and barks echoing around the trio, "Well, that was unexpected."

Elara crumbled to the ground in exhaustion.

Sylvan and Rascal raced to her side, "Elara?!"

Elara: "I'm okay. I promise. Just tired…"

Rascal: "How did you do that?"

Elara, a mixture of relief and exhaustion in her eyes, "Yeah Sylvan, how did I do that? It was like I could feel their pain, their anguish…"

"I actually don't have an answer for you," Sylvan, a reassuring smile on his face, "Your powers are growing. They're surpassing those that came before."

Rascal: "Well that was enlightening as ever. I say we find a sturdy patch of ground and eat. I don't know about you guys but I am starving!"

The trio begin to make their way towards a safe spot to make camp for the night.

Back in his lair, Malachar roared in anger, catapulting his cauldron to the other side of the room, "IMPOSSIBLE! THAT GIRL IS NO EMBERLYN! What is she?"

Nightshade narrowly avoided the splashing of the cauldron's contents, "Master, all this yelling isn't good for you…"

Malachar: "What's no good for us is that any day now that *thing*, and her two sidekicks will be bursting at our door."

Nightshade trembled from his perch against the cave wall, "What are we going to do, Master?"

Malachar: "GET ME FENRIR, GET ME BAYONNE, GET ME EVERY DAMNED SOUL WE HAVE LEFT! IF IT'S WAR THEY WANT THEN WE'LL RELEASE EVERYTHING WE HAVE!

Nightshade: "Yes Master. Right away Master."

Malachar: "NOW!"

Letting out a startled squeak Nightshade fell from his perch and frantically flapped his wings beginning his search for the generals of the unholy hoard.

Malachar watched Nightshade fly away thought to himself, *I think the time has come to call upon the Fates. I need answers and I need them now!*

Malachar made his way and stood in the center of a vast stone altar, he raised his arms, and the candles, scattered throughout the cavern, were drawn toward him.

With a sweeping gesture, Malachar arranged the candles in a perfect circle around him. The cavern's atmosphere thickened with anticipation, and the shadows seemed to coalesce around the shaman, amplifying his power.

Malachar's voice began to echo through the cavern:
"In the veil of shadows, where destiny hides,
I beckon the Moirai, with powers abide.
Candles aglow, like stars in the night,
Illuminate the path, in the ethereal light.

Threads of fate, woven in cosmic loom,
Guide your presence, dispelling the gloom.
From realms unknown, where time is entwined,
I call upon you, in shadows confined.
By the moon's gentle glow and the stars' silent plea,
Awaken the weavers, the Moirai, to me.
As candles unite in this mystical dance,
I summon the sisters to share their advance."

An eerie stillness settled over Malachar's lair. Suddenly, a cold wind swept through the cavern, extinguishing the candles and a trio of ethereal figures materialized before the sorcerer — the Moirai...

Atropos, the eldest, her voice like the rustle of ancient parchment, spoke with a measured tone, *"You DARE summon us Shaman?"*

Malachar, though normally brimming with arrogance, felt an unsettling shiver crawl down his spine. He gestured defiantly, attempting to conceal his unease, "I seek your wisdom, oh wise Moirai."

Lachesis, her eye a pool of infinite wisdom, intoned with an air of foreboding, *"In the shadow of your ambitions, a tempest stirs, a force beyond your reckoning. The very darkness you seek to wield shall become the harbinger of your undoing."*

Malachar's eyes narrowed, a flicker of uncertainty betraying his confident facade, "What nonsense is this? I control the shadows; they do not control me."

Clotho, her voice a haunting echo, whispered words that sent a chill through Malachar's core,

   "As the moon's glow wanes, stars align,
   A choice unveiled, in destiny's design.
   A path to salvation or the abyss,
   Beware, shaman, in balance you reminisce."

Malachar, unable to mask his growing desperation, dropped to his knees before the Moirai, "Tell me, wise sisters, how can I avert this impending doom? Offer me guidance, grant me your wisdom!"

The eldest Moirai, her eye stern and unforgiving, responded in a haunting rhyme,

   "In mortal matters, we intervene not,
   For destinies entwined, we dare not disrupt.
   Threads woven by fates, your path is your own,
   Face the shadows, or be overthrown."

Malachar, beads of sweat forming on his forehead, pleaded with a tremor in his voice, "I beg of you! I am desperate; I implore you for aid!"

The Moirai shook their heads in unison, their expression unwavering,

   "No plea can sway what weavers dictate,
   The course is set, the die in fate.
   Walk your path, in shadows vast,
   Face the consequences, for they are cast."

As the Moirai dissolved into the shadows, leaving Malachar

kneeling in the cold darkness of his lair, a sense of dread lingered in the air.

The cryptic prophecy echoed in his mind, a haunting refrain that left him grappling with the uncertainty of his destiny. With a heavy heart, Malachar rose to his feet, his once unshakable confidence now replaced by a gnawing fear of the unknown. The Moirai had spoken, and the threads of fate continued their relentless march toward an uncertain future.

Chapter 10

Deep within the cavern, Nightshade had rounded up Bayonne, Fenrir, and the others. The fires and torches blazed and flickered as if in anticipation of what was to come.

Stepping forth from the shadows, Malachar materialized with an air of ominous grandeur. His intense gaze traversed the assembly of his horde, and his commanding voice echoed through the cavernous expanse, "Behold, my loyal minions, my cohorts of darkness, and my soulless assembly of misfits and miscreants. The hour is upon us to unfurl our wings and unleash our relentless assault."

Fenrir: "My wolves and I are yours to command."

Bayonne: "My coyotes are ready and willing, Master."

The demons growled in the dark as the souls moaned their pitiful cries in answer to their masters' call to arms.

Malachar, his eyes aflame with arrogance, raised his staff, the shadows dancing around him like obedient servants. "Minions of the abyss, creatures of the night! Today, we stand at the precipice of glory. Today, we usher in an era where shadows shall consume the feeble light. Our destiny is written in the tapestry of darkness, and you are the instruments of its unfurling."

Nightshade cackled with delight, the demons hissed in anticipation, and the lost souls moaned in eerie unison. Bayonne's eyes glowed with a predatory light as Fenrir and the wolves let out a bone-chilling howl.

Malachar: "Elara and her pitiful companions dare challenge our might. They believe in the feeble power of light and unity. But remember my minions, their light is but a fleeting candle, easily snuffed out by the dark. Today, we crush their hope, extinguish their feeble flame, and claim dominion over this realm!"

The dark echoes of Malachar's speech reverberated through the cavern. Malachar's eyes narrowed as he gazed at his horde, "Pray you don't disappoint me."

Meanwhile on the edge of the Obsidian Swamp, Sylvan approached Elara, his eyes reflecting the sincerity of his words. The murmurs of the swamp and the distant echoes of the approaching battle provided a haunting backdrop to their conversation.

"Elara," Sylvan began, his voice a gentle rustle among the leaves, "do you see the path that fate has woven for you? The very fabric of the woods seems to whisper tales of your journey, a journey that has led you from the gentle caress of Everwood to the looming shadows of this forsaken swamp."

He placed a comforting paw on Elara's shoulder, his touch carrying the warmth of both camaraderie and mentorship, "I want you to know, my dear, that in the short time we've known each other, I've watched you grow. From the moment you entered these woods, so unsure and burdened by your doubts, to now standing on the cusp of a battle that will decide the fate of us all. You've come so far, farther than even you might realize."

A soft smile played on Sylvan's lips, "Your gift, Elara, is more than just the manipulation of vines and rocks. It's hope. Before you had entered this forest, I had lost hope. The woods, once a sanctuary, had become a prison under Malachar's influence. But then, you arrived, like a spark in the darkest night, rekindling a flame I thought was forever extinguished."

Sylvan's eyes gleamed with pride, "You've faced trials, challenges that would have broken others, and yet, here you stand. Your spirit, your determination, it's a testament to the strength within you. Amelia and Erik would be proud. I am proud. You give people hope, Elara, and in these shadows, that hope is a beacon that can guide us through the darkest of times."

He took a step back, kneeling respectfully, "I, Sylvan, Gatekeeper of this Realm, now stand before you not as a mentor, but as an ally. I've seen your power, your courage, and your heart. Today, you are not just Elara, a girl who wandered into the woods; you are the Champion of the Forest. I will follow you anywhere, for in you, I have found a leader, a friend, and the true guardian this forest deserves."

Rascal, lounging on his log munching on an apple, "That goes for both of us, kid."

Sylvan exasperated, "Will you stop eating!"

Rascal: "What? I'm hungry. Besides, you need a balanced breakfast before marching into battle. You can't face impending doom on an empty stomach."

Sylvan turned away from Rascal, "You need to make sure you have enough for the journey home."

Rascal looked at Sylvan's back, "Home? What are you talking about? I'm not going home. I've been here since day one. I'm not leaving you or the kid now."

Elara looked towards Sylvan before turning to Rascal, "I'm going to make sure we have everything packed up and douse the fire." Elara set about packing up camp, leaving Sylvan and Rascal to talk.

Sylvan turned to face Rascal, his eyes blazing, "You don't belong here Rascal. She's the Champion, and I'm the Gatekeeper. This is our battle, not yours. You need to go home."

Rascal, feeling his anger rise, "I'm just as much a part of this as you are, Oh Mighty Gatekeeper. If YOU haven't noticed buddy you aren't much of a Gatekeeper right now!"

Sylvan finally broke as a tear escapes his eye, "I CAN'T LOSE YOU!"

Rascal's eyes widened as he watched Sylvan.

Sylvan: "I can't Rascal. Not again. You're all I have left. I can't let you do this."

Rascal moved closer to Sylvan, "Then don't send me away, we're brothers. We're meant to be together. So let's do this. Together." placing his paw on Sylvan's shoulder, "I know why you left. I know why you had to. It's your job. Dad trained you well. But he trained me too. Don't let his teaching be in vain. Together we are stronger."

Sylvan embraced Rascal, squeezing him tight, "If you die on me out there, I'll bring you back and kill you myself."

Rascal chuckled softly, "Likewise."

Elara came back to where the brothers embraced.

Elara her tone teasing, "Aww we're hugging it out. I knew you could do it! Now, let's go! We have a battle to win!"

The trio approached the cavern as Malachar gazed down upon them. The horde, silent sentinels, at the ready, awaiting their Master's call.

Elara stepped forward, facing her foe, her voice cutting through the ominous silence, "Malachar, this is your final chance.

Surrender your staff, release your hold on this realm, and we might let you live."

Malachar, looking down and chuckling, responded with contempt, "You overestimate your worth. I have an army, you have two woodland creatures. Do you think you stand a chance?"

Elara: "At least I'm not hiding in a hole like a coward. What's the matter? Too scared to face me alone? You're right. There are only three of us against all of you, but we will emerge victorious regardless."

Malachar snarled, "Insolent child! You'll regret those words! GET THEM!"

A deafening roar, reminiscent of a hurricane's mighty fury emerged. The very ground quivered beneath the relentless onslaught of countless paws. Each step unleashed a torrent of chaos, as razor-sharp claws tore into the Earth, propelling the dark horde with a relentless determination toward the trio.

Sylvan picked up a thick branch, "Get ready."

Rascal picked up another branch, "Til the end brother, may the best raccoon win."

Elara: "Let's end this."

Slamming her foot down, Elara created cracks in the Earth that gave way to immense craters for the wolves and coyotes to fall into; while with her arms outstretched she dismantled the souls and demons creating shields and barriers to keep them at bay.

Elara shouted, "I've got them. Take care of the rest."

Rascal and Sylvan shared a look before Rascal raised his branch, charging at Bayonne, "Let's dance!"

Rascal, armed with nothing but a sturdy branch, faced Bayonne in the clearing. The air was thick with tension as the two adversaries locked eyes.

Rascal, relying on his quick wit and agility, darted around Bayonne with the grace of a seasoned acrobat. He swung the branch with precision, aiming for Bayonne's legs, but the coyote evaded the blows with uncanny agility.

"Come on, Bayonne! Is that the best you've got?" Rascal taunted, his words laced with a playful arrogance.

Bayonne, snarling, lunged at Rascal, jaws snapping. Rascal leaped to the side, narrowly avoiding the attack. He countered with a swift strike to Bayonne's hindquarters, prompting a yelp of frustration.

Meanwhile, a chorus of eerie howls pierced the air, and a pack of wolves emerged from the shadows, their eyes gleaming with a predatory glint.

Sylvan, facing the encircling wolves, spoke with a measured calmness, "Fenrir, show yourself. Let's settle this."

From the pack, a massive black wolf stepped forward, his eyes locked onto Sylvan. It was Fenrir. The other wolves formed a ring around them, anticipating the impending clash.

Fenrir, his voice a low growl, retorted, "You're a mere shadow of your former self, Sylvan. What chance do you think you have against me?"

Sylvan, though lacking his once-potent magical abilities, squared his shoulders defiantly, "Magic or not, I'll face you on my terms. One-on-one, without your pack."

Fenrir's lips curled into a snarl, he nodded in agreement. The other wolves watched with tense anticipation, their breath forming misty clouds in the cold air.

The two opponents circled each other, eyes locked. Sylvan's eyes, once vibrant with magical energy, now reflected the weariness of a warrior who had faced both triumphs and defeats.

Fenrir lunged, swift and powerful. Sylvan, relying on the instincts honed through years of combat, sidestepped the attack, delivering a swift kick to Fenrir's flank. The black wolf staggered, momentarily off balance.

Sylvan seized the opening, launching a series of agile strikes. His fists connected with Fenrir's side, each blow resonating with the echo of countless battles. Fenrir, recovering from the surprise assault, retaliated with a sweeping tail swipe that sent Sylvan sprawling.

Undeterred, Sylvan regained his footing. As Fenrir lunged again, Sylvan, with a swift roll, avoided the attack and slashed at Fenrir's hind leg. A growl of pain escaped Fenrir, but the primal fury in his eyes burned brighter.

The dance continued, Sylvan, utilizing his speed and agility to outmaneuver Fenrir. Blows were exchanged yet, with each strike, Sylvan felt the weight of his diminished powers. The once-commanding force of nature now grappled with the limitations of mortality.

Fenrir, relentless and cunning, anticipated Sylvan's movements. A powerful bite grazed Sylvan's shoulder, eliciting a pained grunt. The confrontation took on a rhythm of snarls and strikes echoing through the night.

Despite his resilience, Sylvan found himself outmatched. Fenrir's sheer strength and primal instincts were formidable adversaries. The black wolf seized an opportunity, sinking his fangs into Sylvan's side. Pain flared through Sylvan, but he pressed on.

With a sudden, ruthless motion, Fenrir lunged again, this time clamping his jaws around Sylvan's neck. The forest echoed with a guttural snap as Fenrir broke Sylvan's neck.

As Sylvan's lifeless body crumpled to the ground, a fierce rage ignited within Elara's heart. From a distance, she had heard the confrontation, and a wave of grief and rage washed over her. Charging through Malachar's horde, Elara unleashed her powers full force. Sending wolves, demons, and souls alike out of her path, Elara cried out, "Sylvan! NOOOO!"

She cradled him to her, "You're going to be alright Sylvan. I'm going to fix you. I can fix this. I can…I can't fix this…Don't leave me…"

Sylvan opened his eyes, raising his paw to cradle Elara's cheek. He smiles softly before taking his final breath. His paw fell and as it does, so does Elara's control.

Turning her face towards the heaven's Elara cried out, "MALACHAR!"

Rascal, hearing Elara's broken cry, turned to look. As his eyes took in the image of Elara cradling Sylvan's body, pain gripped Rascal like a vice. Bellowing out his rage and heartbreak, Rascal turned to face Bayonne, teeth bared, " Let's finish this!"

The tide began to turn as other coyotes emerged from the shadows. Bayonne signaled to his pack, and the chaos of battle unfolded.

Rascal, outnumbered, relied on his agility to stay one step ahead. He hopped onto the back of one coyote, using it as a makeshift steed. Rage filled his eyes as he swung his branch, knocking down a couple of the advancing coyotes.

The coyotes, undeterred by Rascal, regrouped. Bayonne, fueled by a mix of anger and determination, charged at Rascal. With a swift move, Bayonne knocked Rascal off the coyote's back, sending him tumbling away.

Rascal, now disarmed, found himself backed against a gnarled tree. The growling coyotes closed in, their eyes gleaming with predatory hunger.

Rascal closed his eyes, memories of himself and Sylvan echoed through his head, Rascal fell to his knees ready to accept his fate, when suddenly an unforeseen transformation occurred. A radiant glow enveloped Rascal, starting from the tip of his tail and spreading across his entire being. The once-dull blue color transformed into a mesmerizing golden emerald green, shimmering with an ethereal brilliance. His eyes ignited with an otherworldly glow, reflecting the infusion of ancient power.

Rascal: "You guys are screwed now."

The newfound power surged through Rascal, revitalizing his spirit and enhancing his abilities. With a renewed sense of strength, he deftly maneuvered through the coyotes, his movements now a dance of enhanced agility and power. The golden emerald aura that surrounded him became a shield against the coyotes' attacks.

As Rascal fought back against the overwhelming odds, Elara rose from the fallen Gatekeeper, her aura becoming the inferno she felt inside. Turning her gaze to Malachar, her eyes began to glow with the intensity of the sun.

Elara began to walk towards her foe, his minions being thrown aside as if she had a barrier around her preventing them from touching her.

Malachar standing tall exuding an arrogant confidence, he didn't feel, thought to himself, *Nothing is phasing her...she's like a calm before the storm. How is she so calm?!*

Shooting out her hands, Elara commanded the reeds and tall grass to tangle with the souls and demons bearing down on her. She sent them into a tangle of limbs and weeds as she approached Malachar.

Meanwhile, Rascal, now adorned with the radiant aura of the Gatekeeper, danced through the battle with unparalleled finesse. His movements were a ballet of golden emerald light as he outmaneuvered the coyotes, landing blows with a newfound strength that left them bewildered.

The coyotes, once confident, now found themselves on the defensive. Rascal was a force to be reckoned with. He swung his branch with precision, knocking coyotes aside while darting between them like a streak of golden light.

Just as Rascal seemed to have the upper hand, a haunting howl echoed through the woods. The wolves emerged from the shadows. Their eyes glowed with an ominous light as they joined the fray.

Rascal continued to hold his ground. The wolves, sensing a shift in the tide, hesitated as they assessed the situation. Rascal, now facing both coyotes and wolves, sent them flying, showcasing the newfound strength that the gatekeeper's power had bestowed upon him.

However, from the depths of the shadows emerged the demons and lost souls, their eerie presence casting darkness over the scene. The shadows themselves seemed to come alive, intertwining with the spirits as they closed in on Rascal.

The fearless raccoon fought valiantly, but the overwhelming numbers began to take their toll. The coyotes, wolves, shadows, demons, and lost souls converged, creating a maelstrom of chaos around Rascal. The golden emerald glow struggled against the shadows, and inch by inch, Rascal found himself pushed back.

The relentless onslaught tested Rascal's resolve, and despite his spirited resistance, he began to falter.

Elara, her focus narrowed by her rage,was too focused on Malachar to see her struggling friend.

Rascal realizing the danger he was in began to call for help, "Elara! I could use a little help here! Elara!?!?!"

As the dark forces continued their onslaught against the new Gatekeeper, Fenrir emerged from the pack.

Fenrir snorted in amusement, "This is the new Gatekeeper? HA! Don't make me laugh! Sylvan would be ashamed of this pathetic display…"

Suddenly a flaming blue ball slams into Fenrir's jaw sending him flying into the shadows. A wisp surrounded Rascal forming a barrier between him and the onslaught.

Sylvan: "How's that for pathetic!"

Rascal looked up as the blue fireball became the ghostly image of Sylvan, "Am I dead?"

Sorren: "Not hardly, my boy."

Rascal with a shocked expression on his face, "Dad? What is going on?"

Sorren smiled, "You looked like you needed a hand. It's good to see you living up to your full potential."

Rascal looked at Sylvan, "That's it, I got knocked out. I'm in my head."

Sylvan: "I hate to cut this family reunion short, but we do have a war to win."

Rascal: "Yeah, war, let's go…"

Sylvan looked at Rascal, "You handle the wolves and coyotes, we'll handle the rest."

Rascal: "Who's 'we'?"

Sorren turned and whistled. Rascal's jaw drops as a sea of wisps crash into the demons and souls.

Sylvan laughed, "Get going, Oh Mighty Gatekeeper. You have company!"

Rascal turned his attention to the advancing wolves and coyotes, "Let's see what this Gatekeeper thing can do."

With a swift leap, he slammed his paws onto the ground, unleashing shock waves that cascaded through the horde, sending them sprawling in disarray. As his nimble fingers danced through the air, an ethereal transformation unfolded— his hands, once intertwined, parted to reveal the manifestation of a gleaming emerald battle ax.

Sylvan looked on in awe, "I didn't know we could do that…" turning to Sorren, "We could do THAT?!"

Sorren, avoiding a blow from a demon, laughed, "You could have done that the whole time."

Sylvan dismantling a soul, "The whole time?! You could have told me!"

Sorren, throwing his battle ax at the shadows, "I just did!"

With newfound strength coursing through his veins, Rascal surged forward, the emerald weapon, an extension of his determination. The charge was relentless, and the air crackled with the energy of impending conflict.

Amidst the chaos, a fierce resolve burned in Rascal's eyes. The battle ax cleaved through shadows, the verdant glow leaving a trail of illuminated victory. Each swing was a testament to his prowess.

In the midst of the skirmish, a particular growl caught Rascal's attention. A chilling familiarity echoed in the sound, drawing his focus towards a figure emerging from the shadows. Fenrir, the once-proud adversary, now stood as a grim reminder of the battle's toll.

Infuriated by the memory of Sylvan's demise, Rascal's eyes narrowed with a newfound determination. With a snarl, Rascal redirected his path, closing the distance between him and Fenrir. The air crackled with tension as the emerald battle ax gleamed in the darkness. In a whirlwind of fur and fury, Rascal engaged Fenrir, each strike fueled by a vengeful purpose.

Their clash, a dance of adversaries driven by personal vendettas. Rascal's agile maneuvers and calculated strikes proved to be a formidable force. The forest itself seemed to bear witness to the confrontation, leaves rustling in an eerie harmony.

As the final blow was struck, Rascal's eyes bore into Fenrir's, a mixture of triumph and sorrow etched in the gaze. The once-menacing adversary fell, defeated by the wrath of a brother's vengeance. The emerald glow of the battle ax flickered in the aftermath, a silent tribute to the fallen and a testament to the indomitable spirit of the forest's champions.

Rascal's eyes widened as he gazed upward, beholding a vast expanse of radiant wisps shimmering in celestial blue. They danced amidst the murky shadows, a celestial ballet where the embodiment of good clashed with the malevolent darkness. The wisps, like ethereal comets, chased and intertwined with the enigmatic shadows, creating a mesmerizing display of cosmic conflict.

Each wisp, a beacon of azure brilliance, weaved through the shadows, their celestial glow entangling with the ominous tendrils of darkness. The battle between light and shadow unfolded overhead, a dynamic spectacle of radiant wisps ensnaring and dissipating the malevolent obscurity.

The celestial blue flames flickered and coiled, reminiscent of wisps of smoke intertwining with the shadows. Rascal marveled at the intricate dance of opposing forces, the brilliant wisps gradually gaining the upper hand as they unraveled the shadows, one ethereal strand at a time. The cosmic battleground became a canvas of celestial struggle, where each wisp was a brushstroke of luminous defiance against the darkness.

Meanwhile across the battlefield, Elara, her voice broke through the sounds of war like thunder, "You stole everything…"

Without waiting for a response, Elara rose with the Earth and shot towards Malachar bringing with her a tidal wave of vines, branches, and rock.

Malachar conjured shadows that writhed with malevolent whispers. Elara, drawing upon the swamp's essence, summoned roots that entwined with the shadows, creating a pulsating barrier.

The battle between light and shadow unfolded with a dazzling array of magical prowess. Malachar, a master of dark incantations, cast spells that sought to unravel the very fabric of Elara's control.

Malachar unleashed shadowy tendrils that lashed out with malevolent intent. Elara, deftly countered, weaving protective spells that held the shadows at bay. The very ground beneath them quivered with the clash of opposing forces, nature and darkness locked in an intricate dance.

The battleground was illuminated by the eerie glow of Malachar's spells. Shadows danced and twisted, clawing at the very fabric of reality. Elara stood firm, her eyes focused and determined. The air crackled with tension as the sorcerer raised his staff, unleashing a torrent of inky darkness toward Elara.

Elara, undeterred, extended her hands, fingers weaving through the air as luminescent flora surged forth. A radiant glow emanated from the soil, pushing against the shadows.

Malachar's voice echoed through the swamp, "You cannot escape the shadows, Elara. They are the very essence of this world, and in them, you shall find only despair!"

The shadows lunged at Elara, but she stood her ground. With a forceful gesture, she commanded the Earth to surge forward, clashing against the darkness. The clash created a spectacular display of contrasting energies – the brilliance of the Earth meeting the obscurity of the shadows.

Elara's eyes glowed with an intensity that mirrored the radiance of her magic, "The shadows may be formidable, but so is the light that dispels them!"

As the shadows recoiled, Elara pressed her advantage. She moved with a dancer's grace, her movements harmonizing with the swirling currents of magic around her. With each step, she wove intricate patterns, casting waves of bioluminescent energy that dispelled the shadows in their wake.

Malachar, frustrated but fueled by dark determination, intensified his assault. The shadows thickened, swirling around Elara like a tempest. Yet, she stood resilient, a beacon against the darkness.

Elara's will surged forth in a final, brilliant crescendo. The radiant energy shattered the shadows, dispersing them like tattered fragments of night. Malachar, momentarily blinded by the sudden burst of light, staggered backward, attempting to shield himself with his staff.

Elara, seizing the opportunity, advanced with unwavering purpose, and with a final, forceful push, a shard of obsidian materialized, imbued with the strength of the ancient terrain. With a swift and precise trajectory, the obsidian projectile hurtled toward Malachar's outstretched staff.

The impact was thunderous. The obsidian struck the staff with unyielding force, shattering it into irreparable fragments. Malachar recoiled, the remnants of his once-mighty staff falling away. The malicious aura that had emanated from the enchanted staff flickered and dimmed, leaving Malachar exposed and vulnerable.

As Malachar's staff shattered, a blinding burst of radiant energy emanated from the broken fragments. Within that luminous cascade, the imprisoned essence of Borealis was set free, unfurling in a display of ethereal brilliance. The very fabric of the enchanted realms quivered with the release of this ancient and benevolent force.

Simultaneously, the malevolent demons and tormented souls that had been summoned by Malachar dissipated into nothingness, vanishing like shadows in the dawn's light. The once eerie and withered swamps, plagued by the dark sorcery, were instantly rejuvenated. The air, once thick with the stench of decay, now carried the sweet fragrance of blooming flowers. The murky waters sparkled with newfound vitality, reflecting the azure glow of Borealis' release.

As Borealis soared over the battlefield, the wolves and coyotes, sensing the divine aura, fled in awe and fear. The majestic creature's mere presence compelled them to retreat, leaving the battleground in a sudden hush.

Malachar, stripped of Borealis' energy, returned to his original state. His once-vibrant appearance was now drained of vitality, he withered like a wilted flower. The shadows that had clung to him dissipated, leaving behind a husk of the formidable sorcerer he once was. The very essence of the forest rejected him, recoiling from the darkness that had sought to consume it.

The triumphant glow of Borealis illuminated the entire scene, casting away the remnants of Malachar's dark influence. Elara and Rascal stood in awe as the magical restoration unfolded before them, witnessing the power of light triumph over the shadows that had threatened to envelop their world.

The war was over.

Chapter 11

The battlefield stretched before Elara, a scene of destruction and decay painted in the aftermath of the fierce battle. Elara looked up to see Borealis flying over the swamp in the sunshine.

As the first rays of sunlight caressed Borealis, a radiant spectrum unfurled, a living rainbow born from his very essence, stretching gracefully from his wings to tenderly grace the swamp below.

The swamp, once a desolate landscape marred by the scars of battle, now bore witness to a breathtaking transformation. The air was thick with the scent of damp earth, mingling with the sweet perfume of newly blossomed flowers. Shafts of golden sunlight pierced through the dense canopy, casting a warm glow upon the swamp.

The ground, once trampled and torn, now cradled a delicate carpet of vibrant mosses and tiny blossoms. Wisps danced like fireflies weaving between the reed-like grasses that stood proudly once more. The water, once murky and polluted, sparkled with newfound clarity, reflecting the blue sky above.

The trees, once stooped and weary, now stood tall and proud, their rejuvenated leaves rustling in the gentle breeze. Flowers of every imaginable hue burst forth from the rejuvenated soil, painting the landscape in a kaleidoscope of colors. Butterflies, drawn by the sweet nectar of the newly bloomed flowers, fluttered through the air, leaving trails of vibrant hues in their wake.

The distant calls of unseen creatures echoed through the swamp, a symphony of life reclaiming its home. Dragonflies hovered above the water's surface, their iridescent wings catching the sunlight. Amidst the foliage, the occasional splash of a playful creature disturbed the tranquil surface of the swamp.

Borealis descended from the heavens with a grace that seemed to mend the very wounds of the land. As he touched down, wisps swirled around him in a celestial dance. Their luminescence merged seamlessly with his essence, enhancing his form and transforming him from a colossal butterfly to a majestic elk.

Elara, approached the radiant being, "I am Elara, daughter of Amelia and Erik. It's an honor to meet you."

Borealis chuckled, the sound akin to a melody echoing through the rejuvenated swamp, "Ah, Elara, I've known you for quite some time. The honor is mine."

As Elara basked in the celestial glow of Borealis, her attention shifted to Rascal, who cradled Sylvan's lifeless body amidst the lingering echoes of grief. She rushed to his side, Borealis following in her wake.

"Rascal," Elara's voice was a gentle whisper, filled with empathy.

Rascal, tears streaming down his fur, looked up at Elara, a raw pain etched across his face, "He's gone..."

Borealis, his presence offering a sense of solace, approached Rascal, "I am sorry for your loss. Sylvan was a great Gatekeeper and dedicated many years to protecting the forest. He will be missed by all who seek solace here. It is because of Sylvan that this forest had a beacon of hope. A mantle to follow in the shadows that consumed our home."

Rascal looked at Borealis, "Yeah? Well, you can say that again."

Borealis: "His sacrifice was not in vain, and now he has passed the mantle to you."

Rascal: "Why me...I'm not like him..."

Borealis: "You do not see yourself as clearly as he did. When the bloodline diverges, the mantle of the Gatekeeper passes to the one deemed most deserving of the legacy and power it bears by the previous Gatekeeper. Sylvan chose you."

Borealis looked at both Rascal and Elara, "I am forever in your debt for the sacrifices, and bravery that you have both shown throughout your journey. If there is anything that I can do for you please do not hesitate."

Rascal, voice choked with sorrow, asked the question that weighed heavy on his heart, "Can you bring him back? Please, tell me there's a way."

Borealis' gaze held a profound sadness, "There is no guarantee that once the soul moves on that I can summon it back."

Rascal jumped to his feet, "But he hasn't moved on! He's a wisp. He's still here… Please… Tell me we can at least try…"

Borealis: "We can attempt to bring Sylvan back, but there is a price. The mantle of the Gatekeeper must be passed back to him. You, Rascal, will have to relinquish the powers you hold."

Rascal, without hesitation, declared, "I don't care about being Gatekeeper. I want my brother back."

Borealis positioned himself in front of Sylvan's body. His luminous presence projected a comforting glow.

With a deliberate and graceful movement, Borealis lifted his majestic antlers high, his energy resonating through the air. The atmosphere crackled with the anticipation of something extraordinary as the wisps gathered, forming a delicate halo around him.

Simultaneously, Rascal and Sylvan began to float, their bodies suspended in the ambient magic that permeated the air. The emerald glow, once emanating brilliantly from Rascal, gradually detached from him. It moved with a mesmerizing dance toward Sylvan's lifeless form.

As the magical essence traversed the space between them, a profound transformation unfolded. Rascal's fur, once aglow with a radiant emerald hue, dimmed back to its original dull-blue shade.

Meanwhile, Sylvan's fur, starting from the tip of his tail, underwent a breathtaking metamorphosis. The once-brown fur transitioned seamlessly into a resplendent emerald green, a manifestation of the magical energies at work.

The enchanting dance of magic continued, the emerald glow ascended Sylvan's body, each strand of magic leaving behind a revitalizing touch. As the wisps circled Borealis, a ghostly mist seemed to move through the air towards Sylvan's body. The mist flowed through Sylvan and his chest rose and fell as if taking a deep breath. The ritual reached its crescendo, and both Rascal and Sylvan's bodies gently descended back to the ground.

With a final shimmer, Sylvan's fur reverted to its original brown hue. The swamp, bathed in the ambient glow of Borealis' magic, bore witness to the renewal of life. The once-still bodies now held the promise of a second chance, a testament to the mystical forces that had interwoven fate.

The swamp itself seemed to hold its breath, the air pregnant with anticipation. Rascal crawled to Sylvan, "Sylvan… come on… It's time to get up…you gotta open your eyes.."

Sylvan remained still as Rascal curled himself around him.

Rascal, crying, pulled Sylvan to his chest, "It didn't work…I'm sorry Sylvan…"

Sylvan mumbled into Rascal's chest, "Rascal..I…need to breathe."

Pulling back Rascal stared at Sylvan, "Did you just…"

Sylvan's eyes fluttered open, the spark of life returning to them. The deep hazel became a glowing inferno of amber as the emerald hue broke through from the dark brown fur over his body.

Sylvan took in his first breath, looking down at himself, running his paws over his body before focusing on Rascal, "I couldn't breathe you overgrown hairball."

Rascal, tears streaming down his fur, "You're back! It worked!"

Sylvan smiled as tears filled his eyes, "You gave up being Gatekeeper for me…"

Rascal: "Don't flatter yourself, I didn't want the responsibility."

Rascal, overcome with emotion, embraced Sylvan tightly. Then stepped back hitting Sylvan.

Sylvan, smiling through tears, replied, "What was that for?"

Rascal: "I told you if you died I'd find a way to bring you back and do it myself." Throwing another punch, then hugging him tightly, "You're not allowed to leave me again."

Sylvan returning his brother's embrace nodded, "I won't Rascal. I promise."

Elara: "Sylvan!" racing to him, Elara crashes into him, wrapping her arms around him tightly, "Don't ever scare me like that again! I don't know what I'd do if I didn't have you to help keep Rascal in line."

Rascal: "Hey, in my short time as Gatekeeper we won the war."

Sylvan chuckled, ignoring Rascal's comment, "It was not my intention, Elara."

Elara through tears, "I'm glad you're back. Please don't leave again."

Sylvan pulled back to wipe her tears away, "I won't."

Sylvan looked past Elara to where Borealis stood.

Moving past Elara and Rascal, Sylvan knelt before Borealis, "Great Guardian, I thank you for bringing me back."

Borealis: "It is I that should be thanking you Sylvan. I'm just glad to see that you're back, once a soul crosses to the other side, not even I can guarantee that they can return."

Rascal: "You just didn't want to leave us."

Sylvan turned to face Rascal, crossing his arms, "I couldn't exactly leave you in charge of Elara's training and well-being, could I? She'd be running off on dangerous quests! The trouble the two of you could get into, the possibilities are endless!"

As the brothers continued to bicker, Borealis turned to Elara, his eyes reflecting gratitude, "Champion, I am in your debt, as well. If there is anything I can do for you, do not hesitate to ask."

Elara looked at Borealis, "My parents, Borealis. Can you free them from the Shadow Realm?"

Borealis nodded knowingly, "Of course!" With a radiant glow, he summoned them to the Hidden Grove where Elara's parents awaited her. The air shimmered as the portal to the Grove opened before them.

Elara, her eyes brimming with tears, stepped through the portal into the Hidden Grove. There, amid the ancient trees and flourishing foliage, she found her parents.

Amelia and Erik looked around them, oblivious to their audience.

Erik, looking around him, shocked and shielding his eyes from the blinding light, "We're back...Amelia, we're in the Grove..."

Amelia, looking about her before throwing herself at her husband hugging him tight, "We're home..."

Erik caressed his wife's hair, "We're home."

Amelia and Erik jumped apart exclaiming, "Elara! We need to find her!"

Elara, overcoming her shock, ran over to Amelia and Erik crying out, "MOM...DAD!!!!"

Amelia and Erik spun around to face the group, tearing up, cry out, "Elara!"

Racing into her parent's arms, Elara let the tears and sobs break free.

Amelia cradled her child, "My little dew drop... You're so grown up... My baby..."

Erik held both of his girls to him, kissing the top of Elara's head, "My brave girl. We are so proud of you."

As Elara sought solace and comfort in the arms of her parents, Borealis moved closer to Erik and Amelia, "Welcome Back!"

Amelia looked at Borealis, tears in her eyes, "How is this possible..."

Sylvan beamed with pride, "Elara. She defeated Malachar and broke his hold on the realm."

Amelia gasped and raced to Sylvan, enveloping him in a tight embrace, "Sylvan! Oh my goodness! It is so good to see you!"

Sylvan, struggling against his friend, "Amelia, I still need to breathe."

Rascal laughed, "Nah, we'll just bring you back again."

Amelia pulled back to give Sylvan a concerned look, "Again? What does he mean again?"

Elara took her mother's hand, "You missed a lot Mom. I'll tell you about it later."

Erik nodded to Borealis, "Thank you for bringing us home."

Borealis: "You're back where you belong."

Erik: "Is Malachar truly gone?"

Elara turned to look at her father, "I'm not sure…I broke his staff and Borealis came out of the jewel and I ran to Sylvan…"

Elara's gaze snapped to Rascal and Sylvan, "We have to go after him."

Borealis: "His staff is broken, his forces have scattered, and there is little damage he can do at present. There is much to discuss and to decide right now."

Elara: "I will not let him escape this forest. Mom, Dad, Borealis you stay here. Rascal, Sylvan, and I will take care of this!"

Rascal picked up a branch, "I'm ready kid. Let's go."

Sylvan clapped his hands together manifesting a staff as his hands separate, "As you lead."

Amelia: "Since when could you do that?"

Sylvan: "I could always do it."

Rascal chuckled, "Looks like old dogs can learn new tricks."

The trio race toward the entrance of the Grove as Amelia and Erik look at Borealis in shock.

Borealis chuckled, "You should expect nothing less from the Champion."

As the trio ventured deeper in the forest a profound transformation began to unfold. The once-decaying landscape began to shed the shackles of darkness, revealing a vibrant resurgence of life.

Elara, Rascal, and Sylvan watched in awe as the forest underwent a magical rebirth. The foul rot that had gripped the trees started to recede, revealing the true colors hidden beneath the mire.

Trees, once skeletal and lifeless, now regained their vitality. Leaves unfurled in shades of green, like a painter's palette come to life. The air, once thick with the stench of decay, now carried the sweet perfume of blooming flowers.

Sylvan, with his keen connection to the natural world, couldn't help but feel a surge of energy coursing through the roots beneath his paws.

Sylvan laughed, "Well, this is a sight for sore eyes! The forest is waking up!"

Rascal marveled at the transformation, his eyes widening as he witnessed the rapid revival of the once-dying ecosystem, "This place cleans up nice."

Birds, absent during the dark times, began to return, their melodies forming a harmonious chorus. Squirrels scampered through the branches, and a gentle rustling of leaves heralded the return of life.

Elara: "It's beautiful…"

Sylvan: "I see the forest is already reveling in Malachar's defeat."

Elara: "It's not over yet, Malachar is still out there."

Rascal: "And we'll get him, kid, we'll get him."

Feeling more empowered, Elara, Sylvan, and Rascal continued their journey to the Obsidian Swamp.

The swamp itself was buzzing with life. From the dragonflies over the now clear waters to the frogs croaking on the banks. The wind through the reeds gave way as the trio trekked through.

Coming upon Malachar's lair, Elara stopped.

Sylvan: "Tread carefully, Malachar's desperation knows no bounds, and we remain uncertain of the devious tricks he might unleash."

Rascal looked at Elara, "Sylvan's right kid, be careful," adjusting the branch on his shoulder, "Time to finish this."

Before Elara could respond, an old voice, like that of a warn tome, came echoing from the cave, "Finish this? Do you want to finish this young emberlyn? We will never be finished."

Malachar emerged from the dark, a mere husk of the once imposing figure, his cloak torn and in tatters around his frail body. His eyes still held malice but were sunken into his skull.

Malachar, his voice dripping with malicious intent, "Oh Elara, do you want to know my one regret, not putting an end to you when I had the chance all those years ago."

Sylvan moved to put himself between Elara and Malachar, raising his staff, "You'd never get the chance."

Malachar laughed, a hollow sound echoing off the cavern walls, "And YOU Gatekeeper, have been a thorn in my side. Always meddling. Always disrupting my plans. You and that raccoon of yours."

With a flick of his wrist, Malachar sends Rascal and Sylvan flying to the side of the cavern away from Elara. Sneering,

Malachar moved like a ghost towards Elara. Stopping in front of her, Elara could smell the scent of decay and rot wafting from Malachar. The smell seemed to pour from his very skin.

Elara wrinkled her nose, "Malachar, this ends here. Borealis is free. My parents are free. The forest has already begun to heal, you have no power here."

Malachar pulled back a smirk, "Ah, yes. How are your dear parents, hmm? I'm sure Amelia's as audacious as ever. Unlike your father, just as spineless as a worm, and just as craven. It was so easy to take down the great champion. Her affection for your pitiful father and you was her weakness."

Elara glared, "You know nothing of my father."

Malachar sneered as he revealed the twisted truth to Elara, "And it appears neither do you, my dear, your father was not the honorable man you believe him to be. He was once my devoted apprentice, and together, we ventured into this enchanted realm planning to overthrow Borealis and seize control."

Elara's eyes widened in disbelief as Malachar continued, "Erik's task was to spy on your mother, to delve into the secrets of her magic and Borealis' defenses. Yet, fate intervened. Instead of finding weakness, he found love. Your father, weak in his affections, confessed everything to Amelia and Borealis. A cruel twist of fate, wouldn't you say?" Malachar's voice oozed with a mixture of malice and satisfaction.

Elara: "You're lying!"

Malachar: " Did you believe all those stories that Grammy told you? Haha! Why don't you run back to Daddy and ask him? You're just as weak as your parents, this love that you hold for your family will forever hold you back from achieving the true power you could possess."

Elara, her eyes beginning to glow, "You're wrong. It's love that makes us strong. It makes us fight. Love and light overcome the dark. Like I will overcome you!"

Rearing back, Elara pushed her arms toward Malachar, propelling him backward. With a resounding thud, he collided with the side of the cave wall, emitting a groan. Before he could slump to the floor, the rock coiled around his arms, suspending him along the cave wall.

Elara, eyes blazing, "You stole everything from me. You took everything from this forest. You take and take and take until there is nothing but death and destruction left in your wake! You crave the dark, Malachar?" Obsidian began to grow around Elara's arm stretching out towards her fingertips, becoming a dark blade, "I'll show you darkness."

Malachar smiled a maniacal smile, "That's it child. Give in to your anger, your hurt, give into your darkness. End me here and now and relish in your victory."

Elara rushed to Malachar, letting loose a scream. Suddenly she stopped. Feeling a soft touch on her shoulder, Elara turned to see the emerald eyes of her mother.

Amelia, in a soothing tone, "No, Elara. You're better than this."

Malachar taunted Elara, "What would she know of you? She wasn't there for you."

Amelia to Elara, squeezing her shoulder, "This isn't you. You don't have to do this."

Erik stepped out of the shadows, his eyes as hard as ice, as he looked at Malachar, "Your mother's right Elara. He's not worth it."

Malachar looked upon his old apprentice, "It looks like a decade in the Shadow Realm helped you grow a spine…"

Erik, stepping forward, glared at Malachar, "You may have twisted my path once, but I won't let you manipulate my daughter. Elara, this isn't the way."

Amelia's grip on Elara's shoulder tightened as she spoke with maternal assurance, "Remember who you are, my dew drop."

Elara, caught in a whirlwind of emotions, looked at her parents, then back at the restrained Malachar. The obsidian blade at her fingertips wavered, its dark glow dimming.

Malachar, still suspended, grinned mockingly, "Ah, the family reunion. How touching. But what will you choose, Elara? The path of light or the allure of vengeance?"

As Elara struggled with her inner turmoil, Sylvan and Rascal exchanged a glance. Sylvan nodded at Rascal, who understood the silent communication.

Rascal approached Malachar with a mischievous grin, "You know, Malachar, I've been waiting for this moment."

Malachar sneered, "For what rat?"

Rascal laughed, "For this!" With a swift motion, Rascal punched Malachar in the face.

Amelia and Erik shared a satisfied look, their daughter's moral compass being steered away from the darkness that had haunted their past.

Elara slowly lowered her arm. The obsidian blade receded, dissipating into the ground.

Malachar, now sporting a bruised face, spat out a tooth, "You insolent overgrown furball. Do you think this changes anything?"

Rascal, rubbing his knuckles, retorted, "No, but it sure felt good."

Sylvan, smiling at Malachar, added, "And it was long overdue."

Elara, regaining her composure, addressed Malachar with a steely gaze, "You're right about one thing, Malachar. This isn't over. But I won't become like you."

Borealis, who had silently observed the confrontation, materialized beside Elara. His voice echoed with ancient wisdom, "The forest has endured enough. Let justice be served."

Malachar, now fully aware of his defeat, scowled at the gathering.

Borealis: "Your time in this realm is done, Malachar."

The air crackled with ancient magic as a portal to the Shadow Realm materialized, a swirling vortex of shadows and echoes.

Malachar, weakened and battered, gazed defiantly at the portal, realization dawned on him. Fear flickered in his sunken eyes as the shadows, like voracious snakes hungry for their prey, began to slither out of the opening.

The shadows surged forward to Malachar wrapping around his limbs like insatiable serpents. He squirmed, resisting their grasp, his cries of defiance echoing in the cavern.

Malachar's voice wavered between anger and desperation, "No! You can't do this to me! I am your master! Release me!"

The shadows tightened their grip, unyielding and unforgiving. Malachar, once a formidable force, found himself powerless against the ancient magic that sought to cast him into the abyss.

His pleas grew more desperate as the shadows enveloped him, their inky tentacles reaching into the very core of his being, "Please, I beg you! I can give you more power! More darkness!

Anything you desire!"

Borealis, his gaze unwavering, watched as the shadows entwined themselves around Malachar.

Malachar's struggle intensified, his form almost obscured by the writhing darkness. He clawed at the shadows, his once-commanding voice reduced to guttural pleas, "You can't banish me!"

But the shadows, indifferent to his cries, dragged him inexorably toward the portal's embrace. The edges of the portal flickered with a chaotic dance of dark hues.

The cave resonated with Malachar's final, anguished scream as the shadows converged, fully engulfing him. The portal pulsated with energy, a silent crescendo heralding his descent into the abyss.

Elara looked at Borealis, "Is it really over?"

Borealis nodded, "Malachar may find ways to return, but for now, he is banished."

Rascal teased, "Plus, we already gave Malachar a good beating. What more could you ask for? Except maybe having him as a punching bag, It's a shame we didn't get to keep him. It'd be great stress relief."

Elara chuckled. The weight that had burdened her heart seemed to lift as the forest around them continued to flourish.

Borealis, addressing the group, spoke with a regal tone, "The forest is indebted to all of you. You've faced darkness and emerged victorious."

Amelia, looking at her surroundings, marveled, "It's beautiful."

Erik, placing a hand on Amelia smiled, "Home never looked better."

As the group stood together, united by their triumph over adversity, the rejuvenated forest whispered its gratitude. The leaves rustled in a harmonious melody, and the Sun cast its golden glow upon the newfound life.

Elara, surrounded by her family and friends, felt a profound sense of fulfillment. The chapter of darkness had closed, and a new era for the Enchanted Forest had begun.

Elara, looking at her friends and taking her parent's hands, "Let's go home."

Chapter 12

As Elara, Sylvan, and Rascal stepped out of the Enchanted Forest into the familiar clearing that led to Everwood, they were met with a sight that took their breath away. Everwood, once a town shrouded in gloom, had undergone a miraculous transformation.

The once-dilapidated buildings, now standing proud and restored, had undergone a stunning change. Climbing vines, heavy with blossoms, embraced the facades, their petals dancing in the breeze like a myriad of tiny, joyful sprites.

The air in Everwood was not just filled with the fragrance of blooming blossoms; it was a symphony that enveloped the senses. A delicate medley of lavender, jasmine, and honeysuckle wafted through the streets, creating an intoxicating perfume that spoke of life and rejuvenation. Every inhalation carried the promise of a fresh start, a reminder that the town had emerged from the shadows into a brighter, more vibrant existence.

The fields that encircled the town were a breathtaking mosaic of colors as if an artist's palette had been spilled across the landscape. Rows of sunflowers, their golden faces turned towards the sun, nodded in agreement with the gentle breeze. Lavender fields swayed gracefully, releasing waves of soothing aroma. Neatly plotted rows of vegetables and fruits created a kaleidoscope of hues, from the deep greens of thriving lettuce to the fiery reds of ripe tomatoes.

As the trio traversed the outskirts of Everwood, they marveled at the bountiful harvest that stretched as far as the eye could see. Apple orchards bowed under the weight of plump, rosy fruit, their branches creating arches of natural abundance.

Fields of wheat and barley, now golden in the sunlight, whispered promises of hearty bread and nourishing meals. Crops, once mere saplings, had flourished with life under the warm embrace of the sun. The town's once-barren fields were now a testament to the magic that had returned to Everwood. Bees hummed busily, pollinating blossoms, while butterflies danced through the air, leaving trails of color in their wake.

Everwood, once a town teetering on the edge of decay, now stood as a testament to the resilience of the human spirit and the enchanting magic that flowed through the veins of the enchanted realm. The beauty that surrounded them was not just a visual feast but a reflection of the hope and renewal that had breathed life back into the very heart of Everwood.

Elara, her eyes wide in disbelief, whispered, "Is this… Everwood?"

Amelia grinned as she and Erik stepped out into the sunlight, saying, "Isn't it beautiful?"

Elara nodded in response to her mother as the group walked through the bustling streets, the townsfolk stopped and looked at them in awe, seeing Erik and Amelia for the first time in over a decade.

Erik grumbled, "Great, they're staring at us."

Sylvan looking amused, "Well you have been gone for over a decade."

Rascal: "It could also be the fact that there is a four-foot-tall green squirrel and blue raccoon that can talk."

Suddenly the sweet aroma of baked cookies came wafting through the air as they reached the heart of the town. The family bakery stood as a warm beacon of comfort. Its exterior, adorned with quaint wooden panels and a rustic sign bearing the name *Eudora's Bake Shop* inviting passersby with a promise of delightful treats within.

Amelia held onto Erik's arm, "It's just how I remember it."

Eudora opened the door and flipped the open sign outside.

Elara, unable to contain her joy, ran towards the bakery, "Grandma!"

Eudora turned towards the sound and let out a startled gasp.

Eudora immediately rushed to Elara crying, "Oh my poor child! We need to clean these cuts…and oh look these bruises. I have some paste that will clear those right up. My own recipe. Oh and look at your cloak! It's all torn into tatters..I'll fix it right away. Give it to me right now!"

Elara tried to calm Eudora down, "Grandma, it's ok. I'm ok."

Eudora clutched Elara crying, "I've missed you so much. Oh my goodness, look how much you've changed."

Elara: "There's someone else that wants to see you, Grandma."

Eudora: "And who might that be?"

Elara smiled through the tears, stepping aside to show her parents behind her.

Eudora locked eyes with Amelia. Eudora's eyes welled with tears as she gazed upon her daughter. The wrinkles that etched the corners of her eyes seemed to deepen with the multitude of emotions swirling within.

Her hands trembled slightly as she walked towards them and reached out, fingers brushing against Amelia's cheek as if to confirm the reality of her presence, "Amelia…..is it really you."

Amelia with her eyes tearing up whispered, "Hi Mom…"

Amelia, feeling the weight of the years they'd been apart from Eudora, embraced her tightly. The warmth of a mother's hug, long missed, enveloped them in a cocoon of love.

Eudora: "I missed you so much, not a day went by that I didn't think about you. I love you."

Amelia: "I missed you Mom, I love you so much."

Erik echoed his wife's sentiment, his voice filled with nostalgia, "Do I smell cookies?"

Eudora, swatting at Erik with the wooden spoon she had tucked in her apron, half in jest and half in genuine affection retorted, "Keep your sticky paws off my cookies!"

Erik embraced Eudora, "I missed you too, Ma."

Eudora then turned her attention to Elara, Sylvan, and Rascal.

Sylvan, bowing slightly, "I am Sylvan, Gatekeeper of the Forest. It's an honor to meet you."

Rascal offered a humble nod, "And I'm Rascal, just Rascal."

Eudora, wiping away a tear, smiled at the two newcomers, "Gatekeeper, huh? Elara, you sure know how to pick friends. My bakery is open to all of you. Let's celebrate together."

The lines of worry that had etched her face over the years seemed to ease as she embraced them, one by one. Her fingers lingered on Elara's shoulder, a silent acknowledgment of the months they had been apart and the challenges her granddaughter had faced, "You've brought the light back to Everwood, my little Elara. The town has flourished, and it's all thanks to you and your friends."

Amelia and Erik, following closely behind, shared a look of pride and gratitude. The realization that their daughter's actions had not only saved the forest but also rejuvenated Everwood filled them with a profound sense of accomplishment. The air seemed thick with unspoken emotions as the family stood together, reunited after years of separation.

Eudora, looking at Elara and Amelia, her voice carried the weight of a mother's love, weathered by time and distance, "I missed you both more than words can say. I even missed you, Erik."

Erik, as he munched on a warm cookie, said, "I knew it was only a matter of time before you warmed up to me."

Eudora: "I thought I told you to stay away from my cookies! You'll spoil your appetite!"

Erik moved on to the next delicious treat, "Relax, Ma. I'll still eat. Believe me, I am starving."

Amelia chuckled at her husband and mother's banter as Elara asked, "Are they always like this?"

Amelia: "They're just getting started. It'll be worse now that they have years to make up for."

Looking up, both mother and daughter caught the gaze of Eudora. Tears glistened in Eudora's eyes as she stepped back, holding her daughter and grandchild at arm's length, as if memorizing every feature, "Look at you, both of you. My heart can finally rest knowing my family is whole again."

The reunion continued, filled with shared stories, laughter, and the aroma of Eudora's home-cooked meals. Borealis, watching from a distance, smiled at the heartwarming scene.

Later that night, as Sylvan and Rascal bid their goodbyes and promised Elara that they would see her the next day, the brothers walked back to the forest.

Sylvan, breaking the silence, "Acorn for your thoughts."

Rascal: "Just thinking about the past couple of months."

Sylvan: "Yeah, Amelia and Erik are back, I died, Elara's the new champion, and we're together again."

Rascal: "Yeah, and we brought you back. You couldn't escape that easily."

Sylvan: "Just admit that you missed me."

Rascal, bumping Sylvan with his shoulder, "Not on your life, brother."

Sylvan and Rascal share a laugh as they enter the Heart of the Forest. Borealis stood in his stag form, antlers held high with an air of regality. Bowing their heads respectfully, both Sylvan and Rascal addressed the Guardian.

Sylvan: "Good evening Borealis, is there something we can do for you?"

Rascal smiled, "Make it quick, it's time for some shut-eye."

Sylvan looking appalled, "Rascal, show some respect!"

Borealis chuckled softly, "I'll be sure not to disturb your beauty sleep, Rascal."

Looking between the pair, Borealis said, "We have much to discuss, but not here. Will you accompany me to the Grove?"

Sylvan and Rascal share a look before nodding.

Rascal: "Lead the way."

Borealis stood there, his form radiant. The air shimmered with ancient magic as he transported them to the Grove.

"Rascal," Borealis spoke, the brilliance of his presence casting a soft glow on the surroundings, "Your journey alongside Elara and Sylvan has been a testament to your courage and steadfast loyalty. When shadows threatened our haven, you did not shy away. Your sacrifice, relinquishing the esteemed role of Gatekeeper to bring Sylvan back, is a sacrifice recognized by every rustle of the leaves and the whispering wind."

The great trees seemed to lean in, as if eager to catch every word. Borealis continued, "The gratitude of the forest courses through its very roots, and I, as its voice, express my deepest thanks. You have joined this quest, not for glory, but for the well-being of our home."

His gaze, a radiant constellation in the dimming light, bore into Rascal's eyes. "In recognition of your valor, I extend an offer. Will you accept the esteemed role of Warden of the Hollows? The guardian of this sacred enclave, where the forest beats in harmony with the Hollows and Obsidian Swamp."

Rascal, stunned, stammered, "Warden? Me?" He exchanged a glance with Sylvan, who nodded with a proud smile.

Borealis, his voice resonating with regality, continued, "The Hollows are a sacred part of this realm, and they need a guardian. You have proven yourself worthy. Will you accept this responsibility?"

Rascal, overcome with both shock and honor, nodded, "I—I accept."

Borealis smiled, "Excellent! Tomorrow we shall reconvene and celebrate your new role."

Rascal: "Thank you…"

Sylvan patted Rascal on the back, "Congratulations brother! Let's get some rest. Tomorrow is a big day."

Rascal: "That's the best idea you've had all day."

Rascal and Sylvan left the Grove and made their way home.

Under the morning sun, a magical ceremony unfolded outside of the Hidden Grove, where the trio stood alongside Eudora, Amelia, and Erik. Borealis addressed Elara and Rascal who stood before him, the assembled party witnessing the momentous occasion. "In times of darkness, hope is a beacon that guides us. Each of you, by your actions, has kindled that flame. Elara, you are now the Champion and a defender of this enchanted realm. Rascal, as Warden of the Hollows, you will safeguard the balance of nature."

As Borealis spoke, the air itself seemed to shimmer with the magic of his words. Elara stood with a humble yet determined expression, her gaze meeting each member of the group. Rascal, with newfound responsibility, stood tall, his eyes reflecting a mixture of astonishment and resolve.

Elara's gaze swept over her parents' faces. Amelia and Erik stood proudly with radiant smiles. Eudora sat beside Elara's parents, another beacon of pride and love. Elara felt their pride and stood just a little straighter, smiling back.

Borealis continued, "Hope is the seed from which great deeds grow. You, dear friends, have shown that even in the darkest moments, the light of hope can pierce through. Now, let us celebrate this moment, a convergence of destinies that will shape the future of our enchanted realm."

The forest became a tapestry of magical hues. The air buzzed with energy as Borealis raised his antlers high, and a radiant glow enveloped the group. Elara and Rascal, the new champions of the realm, stood at the center.

Wisps emerged and embraced the duo. Spinning around them like a tornado of celestial light. Elara's amulet began to glow and rise, floating in front of her, the glow intensified as the ancient magic settled inside the new champion.

As the magic surged, Rascal felt an uplifting force beneath him. Slowly, he ascended into the air, his fur changing from a dull blue to a glowing, ethereal blue. His eyes, reflecting the magic coursing through him, radiated with a newfound brilliance.

Borealis, with a final proclamation, declared, "May hope guide your every step. For in hope, we find the strength to shape our destinies."

The scene became a breathtaking display of magic and celebration. The forest echoed with cheers as Elara and Rascal embraced their roles, their connection to the enchanted realm now woven into the very fabric of their beings.

Perched high in the treetops watching the ceremony, was Nightshade.

Nightshade stuttered, "Not good. Not good! Not only do we have the Gatekeeper, but now a new champion AND a warden?? Oh, Master isn't going to be happy…not happy at all."

Releasing the branch, Nightshade began to flutter before catching an updraft and taking to the sky, "I need to tell Master. First, I have to find a way into the shadow realm. Then I need to find Master in the shadows and tell him… yes..that's the plan."

Nightshade cackled into the sky, "Master will be so pleased with me that he'll reward me with my own gooseberry bush, not the green ones, but the delicious red ones. They're my favorite. Yes! Oh, I need to tell him right away….is that a gooseberry bush!?"

Swooping down to dive into a gooseberry bush, Nightshade began to munch on the delicious red berries saying, "I'll find a way tomorrow."